HIGH, WIDE AND DEADLY

From the front of the herd came the sound of gunfire. Slocum spurred his horse forward. The animal was moving swiftly toward the herd.

A shotgun roared in the distance. The loud noise startled the herd. The cattle began to mill around, snorting and pawing the earth.

Slocum's horse rushed past the cattle, cutting along the edge of the herd. Slocum reached down and pulled his Sharps repeating rifle from the scabbard.

He caught site of a rider trapped among a group of milling steers. Fred Tumwater was desperately trying to calm the cattle. He was attempting to hold the herd, not firing back at the four masked rustlers galloping toward him.

"Protect yourself!" Slocum yelled.

Tumwater's face was ghostly white in the twilight.

Slocum snapped the rifle up to his shoulder. He squeezed off a quick shot at the masked riders.

Through the dimness, Slocum saw Fred Tumwater drop low on his saddle. The wrangler pulled his pistol and started to fire.

Slocum started to spur his horse forward, then saw that the other three rustlers had spun around . . .

OTHER BOOKS BY JAKE LOGAN

JAKE LOGAN

HIGH, WIDE, AND DEADLY

BERKLEY BOOKS, NEW YORK

A Berkley Book/published by arrangement with
the author

PRINTING HISTORY
Berkley edition/June 1987

ISBN: 0-425-10016-2

A BERKLEY BOOK ® TM 757,375
Berkley Books are published by The Berkley Publishing Group,
200 Madison Avenue, New York, N.Y. 10016.
The name "BERKLEY" and the stylized "B" with design
are trademarks belonging to Berkley Publishing Corporation.

PRINTED IN THE UNITED STATES OF AMERICA

1

John Slocum and Elizabeth Winston were oblivious to the warm breeze blowing back the curtain on the window of their hotel room in Denver. Their minds were focused on their passion for each other, their bodies entwined atop the sheets of a massive oaken four-poster bed.

Without warning, Elizabeth broke the kiss, and rolled over onto her own pillow. She looked at John Slocum with warm and gentle eyes.

"Anything wrong?" Slocum asked.

"I hate saying goodbye." She laid her head on the muscular smoothness of his shoulder. "All I've ever done is leave the people who mean the most to me. First my parents when we started to Oregon, and now I'm saying goodbye to you."

Slocum took a deep breath and cleared his throat. "Likely we've grown too fond of each other."

She nodded. "Where would I be if you had taken another trail?" A vague wistfulness edged her voice.

Slocum wanted their last hour to be sweet, without tears.

"You'd probably be a white woman in an Indian camp," he said, hugging her close to him. "And the Indian braves would be fighting each other to get you off in a berry patch."

"I'm going to miss you. You say the sweetest things."

"The feeling is mutual."

"How long have we been together?" Her voice was shaky.

"We've been in Denver for three days," he said. "I found you on the trail about a month ago. Look, let's make love for the last time. Then we'll walk over to the stage station, wait there, and pretend to be a man and his wife saying farewell."

"No."

"Why not?"

"Waiting at the station will be too painful."

Then, with a tiny cry of part pleasure, part anguish, she rolled against Slocum. Her arms encircled his body in a passionate embrace.

"Oh, John," she whispered. She opened her legs, reaching out her hand to guide him gently into the moist warmth of her body. She shuddered as he entered, then her legs locked around his body. She began to twist against his throbbing thrusts, moving her body in hungry, swirling motions.

"Ohh!" She moaned. "I . . . love . . . you!"

He drove deep into her flesh.

"I'll never forget you," she sighed.

"My sweet darling." Slocum gently kissed the panting

woman on the forehead, then buried his face into her black hair.

Afterward, they lay with arms entwined and enjoyed the touch of their naked bodies. Haltingly, sometimes stopping to search for words, John Slocum confessed his attraction to Elizabeth Winston.

"I'm going to miss you," he said.

"You can always come east with me."

Slocum shook his head. "I wouldn't fit into that world."

She nodded with understanding. "I have to go back, John. Otherwise I'll stay here with you. And that means I'll never see my mother and father again. I was foolish to marry Kyle Winston, and even more foolish to take off for Oregon with him."

"Everyone makes mistakes," he said. "Don't blame yourself."

"I didn't know Kyle was such a fool."

"This country tests a man."

"And Kyle was found wanting."

"We'd better get dressed," Slocum said.

"Damn!" Her voice was filled with emotion. "I'm going to miss you."

Slocum dressed quickly and sat admiring Elizabeth Winston as she pulled on her petticoat, bloomers, and a high-necked black dress he had purchased for her in Denver.

Slocum had been riding below the Oregon Trail south of the Platte River in western Nebraska. He had found Elizabeth Winston and her lone covered wagon sitting beside a water hole. She had been there for almost a week, hoping for someone to come along. She had almost given up any thought of surviving, had accepted the possibility that she would die.

Through tears, she explained that her husband had argued with the wagon master of their caravan headed for Oregon. An arrogant, rich Pennsylvania man's son, Kyle Winston had pulled his rig out of the line of wagons, and started in a southeasterly direction to return to Independence, Missouri.

One night her husband heard something thrashing about in the darkness beyond their campsite. Unmindful of his wife's warning, the prideful young man picked up his ornate custom-made shotgun and started out into the darkness.

He never returned.

Several days later, John Slocum was riding across the prairie when he caught sight of the white cloth of the canvas-topped wagon stranded by the water hole. He found Elizabeth Winston in a state of shock. She was exhausted by the ordeal of feeding and watering the oxen, and surviving alone on the plains.

Slocum turned the livestock loose and convinced the young widow to abandon the possessions in the wagon. They rode double across the plains and into the bustling frontier community of Denver.

Now, watching Elizabeth Winston put the finishing touches on her attire, John Slocum wondered if he was making a grave error. A man could bed down a lot of women, Slocum reflected, but a good woman was difficult to find, even more difficult to keep.

He liked Elizabeth Winston.

She was a wholesome, healthy young woman with the grit to survive under desperate circumstances.

She was the kind of woman a man could take back to Calhoun County, Georgia, settle down with, and raise a family. But he knew he could never go back. Not after the trouble there. Yet sometimes, like now, he longed for the stability of life where he had been raised. But some restless impulse kept him drifting through the West.

Elizabeth said, "A penny for your thoughts."

"I was thinking about my home in Georgia."

She came over and took his hand. "Go back, John," she whispered. "Don't spend the rest of your life wandering around the frontier. I've grown to love you—yes, love you. I hate to see your life wasted by accepting whatever fate brings you."

"Something makes me keep moving. Anyway, I won't be going back."

"You're trying to get away from yourself and the blood-shed of the War."

"I have to play out my string."

She smiled with understanding.

"If you're ever in . . ."

He kissed her hand. "The first woman I call on will be you."

But he wondered, even as he said it, if he would ever go that far east for a woman—any woman.

The sun vanished behind the Rocky Mountains with a final burst of gold and red. John Slocum, the man from Calhoun County, Georgia, sat with his bare feet propped on the edge of the open window in his room on the second floor of the Tremont Hotel in Denver. He had been sitting there for several hours, feeling the gentle spring wind on his feet, reading a copy of the *Rocky Mountain News*.

He was trying to get the image of Elizabeth Winston out of his mind. Their parting that afternoon had been depressing. John Slocum had mixed emotions about Elizabeth Winston returning to her home in the East.

Slocum gazed through the deepening purple twilight, saw that Larimer Street was filling up with a Friday night crowd. Outside the hotel a gaudy red and blue wagon rolled to a stop. A fancy dressed man began crying that a medicine show would start in a few minutes at a lot near the Denver stockyards.

An aging Negro with skin the color of a walnut clambered up on the wagon seat. He picked the banjo in his hands and sang for the crowd. The Negro was dressed in a red velvet coat, pink pantaloon trousers, and polished black boots muddied from Denver's unpaved streets.

Sighing with impatience at the noise, Slocum rose from his chair beside the window. He pulled on his socks and boots, brushed off his jeans, and changed his shirt. He picked up his hat, slapped it across his leg, left the room, and locked the door. Then he walked down the wooden steps to the hotel lobby.

The clerk was a bespectacled young man dressed in a black wool suit and starched white shirt with a stiff collar. He was bent over a sheet of paper containing columns of figures.

Slocum laid his key on the hotel desk.

The clerk glanced up, his eyes blinking behind the thick lenses of his glasses.

"I better warn you," said the clerk.

Slocum's body tensed. "About what?"

"A man came in and checked our hotel register looking for your name," the clerk said.

"The law?"

"I'm new in town. I didn't see a badge."

"Do you let strangers check your list of guests?"

"Not usually. But you don't disagree with this man. He looked hard."

"How was he dressed?"

"He wore a black and white cowhide vest."

"Anything else?"

"He carried a sawed-off shotgun."

"Much obliged," Slocum said. He wondered if the man was friend, foe, or maybe a lawman.

The clerk smiled nervously. "I figure if someone is snooping after a man, he ought to know about it."

"Thanks." Slocum pulled a freshly minted silver dollar from his pocket and laid the coin on the desk.

The clerk's gaze became fixed on the coin. "You don't have to—"

"Let me know if he comes in again," Slocum said.

"Thanks a lot," called the clerk as Slocum turned away from the desk and walked out of the lobby into the crowded street.

The costumed Negro was perched on the wagon seat, picking a melodic tune and drawing a sizeable crowd. Drovers, buffalo hunters, teamsters, a handful of uniformed soldiers, and several farmers were gathered for the free show. While the Negro amused the crowd, the fancy dressed man was giving out tickets to the medicine show out by the stockyards.

Slocum walked down the street to the Paradise Saloon. It was crowded and dimly lit, a place for serious drinkers. The establishment was filled with men who made a business of drinking whiskey on a daily basis.

There was some laughter, and lots of talk about long-term drinking. The crowd, mostly men, discussed epic drinking bouts, bizarre happenings while under the influence, and hangovers that defied medical science.

A squat, mustachioed bartender in a white shirt took Slocum's order for a beer. "Good choice," said the bartender, holding a thick glass mug under a beer tap. "We got the best brewery west of Chicago. The beer is better than most of the slop you'll find out here."

"How much?" asked Slocum.

"A nickel, and that entitles you to the free lunch."

The bartender set a large, foaming mug of beer on the bar.

Slocum paid for the drink and sipped the foamy liquid. The beer was tasty. It had a thick flavor of hops without the flat staleness of beer found in many cowtowns.

Slocum wondered about the man with the sawed-off shotgun. Walking around the streets of Denver with such a weapon was asking for trouble. Slocum also wondered how the man had come to know his name.

John Slocum felt at home in the Paradise Saloon. Around him, elbow to elbow, men were on their way to getting drunk. That was their only intent, and as long as none called him out, he could grant them that. No skin off his nose.

An old man in tattered homespun trousers and a buckskin shirt was unconscious under a table, mouth open, eyes closed. A good old boy who had one too many and passed into a state close to death.

A small hand touched Slocum's wrist. He turned.

A slender woman with a shapely body stood beside him. Her painted lips were opened by a smile that seemed frozen on her face. She wore a red satin gown that was cut low to reveal ample breasts. Long red hair fell back, sprawled over her bare shoulders.

"I'm Rosalie McDonald," the woman said. "Want to buy me a drink?"

John Slocum's gaze moved up and down her body. "What's your poison?"

"Whiskey and water." Her eyes were large and bright, her skin smooth beneath the thick layer of white powder. A hint of strength and health lingered in her body, although her throat was slack with the weakness of a woman who drank too much.

Slocum ordered the drink. Rosalie McDonald sighed contentedly when it was placed before her. "Here's to a party tonight," she said, raising the shot glass.

Slocum grinned. "You're a very direct woman."

"Business is business, honey. A girl has to eat."

"We could go to my hotel room," Slocum said.

"I live right upstairs, honey. No need to waste time walking someplace else."

Slocum recalled some of the great beauties he had bedded down. Actresses, dance-hall girls, Indian princesses, enough whores to fill a large valley. There had been women of every size, weight, and degree of sexual desire. Some possessed inner resources that made them special, made a man remember them long after the pleasure was gone.

He wondered if Rosalie McDonald had the qualities of a winner.

"Want to grab a table?" she asked. "There's one in the back."

Slocum picked up his beer and followed the woman through the crowd. She led him to a small table near the back door of the saloon. Slocum took a chair that placed his back to the wall.

He decided not to bed down Rosalie McDonald. Somehow, going to her room, paying for her services, would soil his memory of the afternoon's lovemaking with Elizabeth Winston.

"This place gets crowded," he said.

"We got a good business." Rosalie sat down near Slocum and rested her hand lightly on his leg. "Now, what is on your mind?"

Slocum raised his finger to his lips. "Be quiet for a moment, honey. This is a historic occasion."

"It is?" Rosalie McDonald looked confused.

"I'm falling in love."

A gritty hardness flickered in Rosalie McDonald's eyes. "Don't josh me," she said huskily. "The price is five dollars. That gets me however you want for twenty minutes."

"Honey, I think you may be the woman of my dreams."

"The price is still five dollars. Twenty-five dollars and you can sleep with me until morning."

"You have a beautiful body."

"Forget the compliments, honey. Do you have the money?"

"Most girls don't charge me," Slocum lied, teasing the woman. "They've even been known to pay *me*."

Rosalie McDonald did not question his statement. "You find dumb Nellies everywhere," she said in a serious tone.

"But not the long-haired red-headed woman at the Paradise Saloon?" Slocum raised his eyebrows in a questioning manner.

"Right, galoot, you got to pay Rosalie."

"Maybe I'm broke," teased Slocum.

Rosalie McDonald's face took on a sudden look of emptiness. "So long, cowboy," she said, rising to her feet.

"What's the hurry?" Slocum reached for her wrist.

Rosalie pulled away from his grasp. "You're poison, mister."

"I was teasing."

Rosalie moved away. "Tell that to the two men who just came through the back door."

John Slocum turned and saw two men standing by his table.

Both men held sawed-off shotguns.

The ugly weapons were aimed at John Slocum's head.

2

It was not the greatest moment in John Slocum's life. He stared at the barrels of the two sawed-off Greener shotguns. They looked like the black mouths of death.

Slocum took a deep breath. He blinked.

The two men in black and white cowhide vests looked exactly alike.

They were identical twins, wearing matched clothes and holding a matched set of shotguns. The two men were tall, about forty-five years old, wearing blue twill trousers and gray shirts under the fancy cowhide vests. Their hats were matched: two dust-colored low-crowned sombreros with leather thongs.

The two men had dark, quick eyes deep-set under dark, bushy brows. Their faces were weathered from exposure to the sun and wind. Their lumpy jowls hung down from high cheekbones, ending in chins that were slightly receded.

The twins moved with the untroubled motions of men who were used to having their orders obeyed. Slocum decided they were not saddle bums or drifters seeking vengeance for some real or imaginary slight.

Slocum took in their appearance, remaining motionless.

"Place your hands on the table," said one of the men.

"Slowly," added the second man.

"We're the Bannerman boys," said the first man. "I'm Frank Bannerman."

The other twin added, "And I'm his brother, Luther. Reckon we want to be sure we got the right jasper. Are you John Slocum?"

Slocum nodded. "Folks call me that."

Luther Bannerman smiled at his brother. "Reckon you called it right again, Frank. I would have bet my honor he'd be upstairs with a fancy woman. 'Pon my soul! I'm getting feeble-minded."

Frank Bannerman smiled at his brother. "Don't talk foolish. This jasper may've been planning to do that later."

"I guess you lose, friend." Luther Bannerman gave Slocum a wide grin. "Trouble with postponin' ever'thing is you might never get a chance to catch up."

Slocum looked at the Bannerman twins with a confused expression.

He asked, "Just what is it that you boys want with me?"

"Oh, dangnation, we been jawing too much to tell you," said Frank Bannerman. "You do the honors, Luther."

Luther stopped smiling. "We're deputies. The high sheriff wants to talk with you. Maybe we better explain. Sheriff heard you was in town. We've been hunting all evening for you. Reckon we've been in every saloon in Denver, some of them two and three times."

"Ain't pleasant visitin' saloons when a man believes in temperance," added Frank. "Now, Luther, we don't want to spook this feller. Let's lower our guns and be friends."

The twins shoved their Greener shotguns into hand-tooled holsters tied to their left hips.

Tension drained out of Slocum's body. He flexed his shoulders to ease the muscles back to normal.

"You use those cannons to greet everyone?" Slocum asked.

Luther Bannerman shook his head in a negative motion. "Nope."

Slocum asked, "Then why pick on me?"

"Your reputation ain't the highest."

Frank nodded. "Some folks'll say you're downright dangerous."

"'Sides that," Luther said, resting his hands across the table from Slocum, "we ain't really mad at you. You oughta see us when we're riled up."

"I'll pass on that spectacle."

"Most folks generally do," said Luther. He dropped down in the chair left vacant by Rosalie McDonald's departure. "You gonna be a nice feller?"

"I am at your beck and call." Slocum watched the twins as if they were rattlesnakes shedding skin.

"That's nice," said Frank.

Luther patted the butt of his shotgun. "These Greeners have a way of getting people's attention."

"They do that," Slocum agreed.

"You wouldn't try to fool us?" Frank looked directly into Slocum's eyes. "Some fellers might decide to pull some silly ol' revolver on Luther 'n' me. 'Specially if they think we're not paying attention."

"I wouldn't do that," Slocum promised.

"We appreciate it." The Bannerman twins spoke in unison.

Frank Bannerman slapped his brother on the shoulder.

"This jasper is right smart for a flatlander."

"Them folk'll get the hang of things pretty soon," Luther said. "Ain't that right, Slocum?"

"You boys ever think of wearing badges?"

"Too bothersome," said Frank.

"Dang right," Luther agreed, pulling back his vest and exposing a shiny nickel-plated star. "Wear 'em on the outside of our vests and they'll snag up on something, ruin our cowhides. 'Sides, most folks know we're deputies. Once we meet a man we stick in his memory."

"I can understand that," Slocum smiled. "I might forget you boys, but the memory of those twin sawed-offs will linger in my mind."

"Lowlanders say that a lot," Luther smiled.

A small group of patrons in the Paradise Saloon had drifted toward the back of the room. Their curiosity had been whetted by the sight of the Bannerman twins pointing their guns at John Slocum's head.

Now the crowd was running on whiskey courage. The Bannermans' shotguns were holstered, so the crowd moved forward to find out what was happening.

More than a few of the drinkers' brains were dulled by alcohol. They held notions that whiskey drinking enhanced their manhood, that each person was a fast draw *hombre* with deadly ability. Several men began to mutter that the Bannerman brothers should be taught a lesson. They mentioned this while standing behind their drinking companions.

The saloon crowd moved with that particular gait of the long-term whiskey imbiber, a peculiar type of slow, uneven step.

The Bannerman brothers acted simultaneously as their hands streaked under their vests. Two Walker Colts appeared in their hands, their barrels pointed at the crowd.

"One more inch and you'll be deader than a doornail," snapped Frank Bannerman.

"You folks better get serious about your drinkin'," snapped Luther.

"Look at these badges!" Frank pulled back his vest.

"Yeah," Luther chimed in. "We're the law."

John Slocum twisted in his chair. He saw the crowd of men drawing away from the pistols. The red-rimmed eyes of the saloon crowd were downcast to the floor as they backed away from the deputies.

The drinkers went back to the bar. Another hour and they would be telling each other how courageous they'd been, or some humorous cowhand would laugh and declare they were all scared out of their wits.

The Bannerman brothers holstered their pistols. They turned to Slocum with apologetic expressions on their faces.

"Pay no mind to that worthless trash," said Frank.

"We get the dregs out here," Luther smiled. "Folks come to Denver thinking the atmosphere is the same as down on the plains. Air's thin in Denver. Affects a man's drinkin' capacity. Two snorts and they're thinkin' of becomin' a *pistolero*."

Slocum's mind was racing. "This meeting with the sheriff has me worried. Does it have anything to do with a poster the sheriff might have?" he asked.

"Tol' you this chile would be bright," Frank told his brother.

"He might do all right here in Denver," Luther answered.

"What about the poster?" asked Slocum.

"We're taking you to meet the sheriff," the twins said in unison.

Luther went on, "When the sheriff wants something,

Frank and me do our best to see he gets it. The sheriff said he wanted you brought in, so we're here to see that you do like he wants."

Slocum asked, "Can I stand up? It helps when I walk."

"Test your legs, Slocum," answered Frank. "Do whatever you want to do as long as you're quiet and careful about it."

"I know." Slocum stood up, flexed his legs. "You don't like flatlanders acting loco."

"You're gonna do real good," grinned Luther.

"Yeah, I win the prize." Slocum smiled at the two deputies.

"Oh, no prizes," said Frank.

"Lordy, no," Luther agreed. "We're not giving out awards this week. See, our wells went dry, our horses took down with the bloat, our dog caught the mange, and our wives are nagging us to death."

"Other than that, we ain't got a care in the world," Frank grinned.

"Now, you follow us, Slocum, and things're gonna go just fine."

They had already started for the back door when Rosalie McDonald came strutting out of the dimness. A whiskey slackness was evident in her features. Her eyes had a dull, misty look.

"Well, evening to you, ma'am," said Luther Bannerman, flicking his fingers to the rim of his hat.

Rosalie McDonald jerked her head in the direction of Slocum. "Is this man under arrest?" she asked.

"No, ma'am." Luther Bannerman looked uncomfortable standing close to Rosalie. His gaze avoided the fleshy orbs riding above her low-cut dress.

Rosalie stepped past the deputy. She stood before Slocum with an ashen face.

"You took up my time, mister," she said, defiantly. "I want to be paid."

Slocum shrugged. "Sorry. I was teasing you."

"I want money." Rosalie's hand came out, palm up.

Slocum pulled a silver dollar from the pocket of his jeans. He laid the coin on Rosalie's hand.

"Fresh from the mint down the street," he said.

"Just a dollar?" Rosalie's voice was raised loud with mock astonishment. "That's like you, jasper. Always trying to get by on the cheap."

Her words angered the man from Georgia. "Spend that with a clear conscience," he snapped. "Whenever I see a silver dollar, I'll think of you. Just like you, Rosalie, a silver dollar goes from hand to hand."

Rosalie's arm swept up in a striking motion.

Frank Bannerman grabbed her wrist.

"Calm down, miss," he said in a firm voice.

Rosalie McDonald's face was clouded with rage. "Slocum's a piece of—"

A bartender came over. "Get back to the customers," he told the woman. He turned to Slocum. "Sorry about anything she said. You know how women get sometimes."

"He said—" Rosalie blurted.

The bartender hissed, "Get back to your customers or you're fired!"

Shoulders slumped, her lower lip quivering with anger, Rosalie McDonald left the group and headed for the bar.

"I was kidding her. Give her my apology when she calms down."

"Forget her," said Frank Bannerman. "We got to go see the sheriff."

John Slocum was shown into the sheriff's office. The Bannerman twins said "so long" and went out to check out a

disturbance at a saloon on Larimer Street called the Bucket
of Blood.

Sheriff Ben Fillmore was a big, strong man—six-foot-
four, two hundred and ten pounds, mostly muscle—and he
was a rare breed: a sheriff who was fair and decent. He was
an honest man who did not filch from the money paid to
feed his prisoners, did not mistreat the men locked up in
jail, and demanded that prisoners be given every possible
courtesy within reason.

During the years John Slocum had wandered from cowtowns to growing frontier cities, he had met a variety of
lawmen. Many were tough outlaws hired to ride drag on
men who were not as mean or brutal. Others were money-
hungry politicians who used the office for every personal
and financial advantage.

Sheriff Ben Fillmore had bucked the odds and remained
his own man. He wasn't a politician, although he came up
for election periodically. He didn't kowtow to the mer-
chants, nor did he kiss the plump rumps of the silver
barons. He wasn't beholden to farmers, cattlemen, the
U.S. Army, stagecoach lines, saloon owners, or any or-
ganized group, lawless or legal.

Sheriff Ben Fillmore treated everyone with the same
courtesy and respect. A millionaire received the same
treatment as a burnt-out whiskey bum stumbling out of a
saloon on Larimer or Curtis Streets. And, thank God, Ben
Fillmore liked being the sheriff of Denver City, Jefferson
Territory, and did not envy other men their wealth, social
position, or behavior.

Slocum sat in a chair facing the sheriff. He was uncomfortable because Sheriff Fillmore had not spoken since the
Bannerman twins had left. Now, Ben Fillmore's gray eyes
were boring into Slocum's face like the stare of an aveng-
ing angel.

Sheriff Fillmore cleared his throat. His right hand came up and smoothed the waxed edges of his gray mustache.

He said, "I hear you're a man who knows how to use a gun."

Slocum shifted in his chair. "I've managed to stay alive."

"What do you want out of life, Slocum?"

"A rich silver mine, a valley of good horses, a fine mansion for a home, and eternal life." Slocum chuckled. "Oh, yeah, add a thousand beautiful women waiting in the bunkhouse."

Sheriff Ben Fillmore's hand formed a fist. Without warning, he slammed the top of his desk.

Slocum blinked, got on guard.

"I asked your philosophy of life," Fillmore snapped.

"Hell, I don't know."

"You fought in the War?"

"Yeah, I did."

"Confederacy?"

"I was Georgia born and reared."

"Understand you had a distinguished record."

"I did my best."

"Why are you drifting around out here?"

"I don't know, Sheriff."

"Ever tried to figure it out?"

Slocum shrugged. "I just kind of go with whatever comes up."

"If you're with Christians, you act pious. If you're with trail tramps you go along with what they do. Is that right?"

"I try to get along, mind my own business, and stay alive."

The sheriff asked, "How many men have you killed?"

Slocum shrugged. "Some men notch their gun butts. I don't."

"But you're fast with a gun?"

"I've been lucky a time or two. I know there is always someone faster. I don't push things."

"Any good at tracking?"

Slocum furrowed his brow. "I can usually find my way home," he answered.

"How long have you been wandering around?"

"Since the War ended."

"You ever hear of Horace 'Strike-It-Rich' Tremont?"

"I'm staying at a hotel he owns."

"Know anything else about him?"

"Just saloon talk. An old man who stumbled across a big silver find."

"Big is right," chuckled Sheriff Fillmore. "Horace Tremont got drunk one night and wandered away from his campsite. He passed out and woke up the next morning on the biggest lode of silver anyone has found. The Comstock lode in Nevada may be bigger. No one is sure."

Slocum had heard a dozen variations of the legend in saloons across the West. Horace Tremont had been a down-at-the-heels prospector whose sudden fortune was envied by every prospector on the frontier. Tremont's unexpected wealth kept men digging, grubbing, and blasting the earth in hope of a similar discovery.

Slocum said, "Most people don't mention that Tremont spent most of his life looking for a rich vein."

Sheriff Fillmore asked, "Did you know he bought himself a wife?"

"Bought a wife?" Slocum grinned. "My side lost the war, Sheriff. Slavery isn't legal."

"I mean his wealth enabled Horace to get a young bride."

"She likes money?"

Fillmore pulled the ends of his mustache. "Actually,

Horace did pretty well. Went back East and come home with Mary Jo, his bride. She is good for Horace. A real lady. Plenty of spunk and high-bred. Not the sort of woman who would marry an old man for money."

"But she married Horace," Slocum pointed out.

"She looks and acts like a lady."

Slocum asked, "What does this have to do with me?"

"Mary Jo Tremont is missing."

"Maybe she got tired of being a rich man's wife."

"She wouldn't leave without telling someone."

"What happened?"Slocum wondered.

"Best as I can figure out she was kidnapped." Sheriff Fillmore looked directly at Slocum. "A gang of hardcases were in Denver on the day she disappeared."

"Anyone I know?"

"They're a sorry bunch of trash," said Fillmore. "They're a pick-up bunch, leastways that is what we're finding out. No permanent headquarters, no real plans, maybe not even a leader. Just a bunch of people riding together and living off the land."

Sheriff Fillmore explained that Horace Tremont had returned home late on the previous evening. His bride was not in their mansion. The old man was told by the servants that Mary Jo had gone into town to shop for goods. She had not returned home when the stores closed.

Slocum asked, "Was she walking or riding?"

"No one seems to know."

"Why are you so sure she was kidnapped?"

"The Bannerman twins spent the morning asking around. One man who hangs around the saloons saw two men pulling a woman into an alley."

"Maybe the man had a whiskey vision."

"That is possible," Sheriff Fillmore agreed. "But it would be like this bunch of saddle tramps to kidnap a woman, not realizing she was a rich man's wife. You know about the underground traffic in women down in Mexico?"

"No, I've missed that."

"Light-haired women with fair skin are sold at a premium down there to wealthy ranchers," the sheriff explained. "The going price is a couple of thousand dollars—not pesos—for a young woman. My gut feeling is that Mary Jo Tremont was grabbed by the gang. They're taking her to Mexico to sell for the highest bid."

Slocum asked, "What does this have to do with me?"

"I want you to bring her back—unharmed."

An agitated expression crossed Slocum's face. "Sorry, Sheriff, I'm not a lawman. Send the Bannerman boys after her. They look as hard as hickory and they're handy as hell with those sawed-off shotguns. If all else fails, they can talk the gang to death."

"In ordinary times I would do exactly that."

"Those Greener shotguns get your interest," Slocum pointed out.

The sheriff smiled. "Those boys are good deputies. But I need them here in Denver. I'm shorthanded, Slocum. A silver strike over in the mountains created a mining camp called Georgetown. The place has gotten wilder than a lobo wolf. The town leaders called on me for help. A third of my deputies are over there trying to calm things down. I can't spare anyone for a wild goose chase."

"So I'm the one to chase down this rumor?" Slocum looked glum.

"I would appreciate it," said Fillmore. "To show my gratitude"—and he spoke the words slowly, with emphasis—"I'm going to give you a helper."

"I ain't said yes."

"You don't have a choice. I'm making you a deputy and your helper will be Pawnee Joe Miller."

"The mountain man?"

"One and the same."

Slocum sighed. "Where do I find Pawnee Joe?"

Sheriff Fillmore smiled. "We got him sobering up in a cell."

3

John Slocum was awakened the next morning by the desk clerk pounding on his door. He yelled a sleepy "okay," got up, poured water from the porcelein pitcher on his bureau into a tin basin. The cold water helped wash the cobwebs from his mind.

After a quick breakfast in the hotel dining room, Slocum went down to the livery stable and waited until his horse was saddled. The liveryman was a fat, middle-aged man with a black beard. He rattled on to Slocum about the rich lode of ore in the Georgetown strike.

"If I didn't have a wife and kids I'd be up there by tomorrow morning," said the stablehand. "Denver is a dying town, mister. The Union Pacific Railroad is going through Wyoming. That leaves Denver high, wide, and off the beaten path. Cheyenne is the next boom town. Railroad stop and everything. Bound to happen. That is why I want to get over to Georgetown and mine some of that ore before it's too late."

Slocum did not comment on the man's observations. His mind was still reeling from the events of the past twenty-four hours. Sheriff Ben Fillmore seemed sure that the gang of drifters had kidnapped Mary Jo Tremont. Slocum suspected the young woman had grown tired of being a rich old man's wife. She had probably hoarded money and was now headed back to her home.

Nonetheless, he guided his horse to the mansion of Horace Tremont. The house sat high on a bluff overlooking the town. Although Slocum was not a student of good architecture, he recognized the house as a monstrous parody composed of geegaws, turrets, ornate curlicues, and tasteless gimmickry.

Slocum tied his horse to a hitching post and walked across the hard plank floor of the porch. His knock was answered by a Mexican woman wearing a frilly white apron over her floor-length black dress. She looked at Slocum with undisguised suspicion.

"Sheriff Fillmore asked me to see Mr. Tremont," Slocum told her.

The woman's expression changed. She led him through the house, past the dining room and into the kitchen.

"He's in there," the woman said, jerking a thumb to an open doorway.

Horace Tremont was seated on the back porch, which was enclosed with thick-paned glass. He sat at a walnut dining table covered with expensive gold and silver platters. Tremont was about seventy years old, if not older, and his thin body was covered by a colorful silk robe.

The skin beneath his chin sagged down like a lifeless appendage. His hands were callused evidence of years he had dug and picked at the earth for riches. His face was veined from too much drinking, but his dark eyes were sharp and alert. His gray hair was plastered back on his skull with a perfumed oil that lingered in the air.

Once the introductions were made, Horace Tremont offered a plate to Slocum. While Slocum was ladling out fresh fruit from a silver-rimmed bowl, Horace Tremont spoke of his wife in reverent tones.

Slocum sat down across from the old man.

Horace Tremont nibbled at a biscuit covered with honey.

"I appreciate your willingness to help me," he said. "Most folks wouldn't do it. They'd think Mary Jo run back to her parents, or maybe took off with a younger man. You think that, Slocum?"

"The thought crossed my mind."

Tremont nodded. "I met Mary Jo coming out of a store in Chicago. I know she's a lot younger'n me. Sure, my money had everything to do with our getting married. A man my age would be a fool to think otherwise. But we've been getting along. Mary Jo is too much of a lady to steal a few dollars and sneak out. And we had an agreement about other men, so's if she wanted them she could have them. She was just supposed to keep it a secret from me."

"Did she see other men?"

Horace Tremont was candid. "Damned if I know for sure. I don't think she did. Now, Sheriff Fillmore told you about finding out some woman was grabbed yesterday?"

"It doesn't seem like much to go on."

"We don't have anything else," said Tremont.

"Chances are mighty slim that gang grabbed your wife."

Tremont nodded. "I've learned to trust my instincts, Slocum."

"Is that how you made your silver strike?"

"Hell no," snorted Tremont. "That was sheer luck. I

was drunker'n a pig and woke up with a godawful head-ache. When it got to where I could see, I found out I'd been passed out on a mountain of silver. Most men lie to themselves, Slocum. I might've shaded the truth a mite in my day, but I never got in the habit of fooling myself. I can make it worth your while to check out this thing about the gang."

"What's worth my while?" Slocum wondered.

"My terms are fair. A thousand dollars if you try to find her. Ten thousand if you find her and bring her back. Is that agreeable?"

Slocum whistled. "More than fair."

Horace Tremont nodded in agreement. "Find my wife, Slocum. Get Mary Jo back to me. You'll have a friend for life. A very rich friend. I'm an old man, and the only person who means anything to me is Mary Jo. She's the reason for me getting up in the morning. I know I'm old enough to be her grandfather, but I love her. In her own way, I think she is fond of me. I don't say she loves me, but she is willing to put up with an old man and do it with a great deal of style."

"You have a painting or drawing of her?"

Horace Tremont reached into the pocket of his silk robe. He fumbled for a moment, then laid a gold locket on the table. "Artist in Chicago did this when Mary Jo was twenty," the silver baron said. "That was a year before we got married. She looks the same today, 'cepting her hair is a bit longer."

Slocum picked up the locket.

"Push that doo-dad on the top," said Tremont.

Slocum pressed a button. The locket opened to reveal a small portrait of a young woman. Slocum's mouth dropped open with astonishment at the flawless beauty depicted in the tiny picture.

"You can see," said Tremont, "why I want her back with me."

Slocum went back to town and left the chestnut Morgan at the livery stable. The stablehand was still talking about going to Georgetown to find his fortune in silver ore. Slocum walked over to the sheriff's office and went inside. The Bannerman brothers were lounging in the office.

"Nothing to do?" asked Slocum.

"Town's quieter than an Injun sneaking up on a Mormon," said Luther.

"We don't get much trouble till the saloons start pouring during the evening," added Frank.

"Then things can get fair-to-middlin' excitin'," said Luther.

"The sheriff in?" Slocum wondered.

"He's gone for a while," Luther Bannerman explained. "Sheriff Fillmore always takes his lunch at home. Afterward he rests for a spell by taking a nap."

Slocum looked displeased. "Did Fillmore mention giving me a partner to hunt down this Tremont woman?"

"Yep," said Luther.

Frank nodded solemnly. "That would be Pawnee Joe Miller."

"Where do I find him?"

"Nothing to it," grinned Luther. "We just go back in the jail and rattle the bars on his cage."

"He's still sleeping it off?" Slocum asked.

"When Pawnee Joe ties one on . . ." Frank paused. "Well, we was lucky this time. He just come to town for some serious drinking. Couple drunks back the old man got on a mean drunk. Feeling sorry for himself, I expect. Me and Luther figure he's just getting old and cranky. Folks'll get that way, you know. 'Specially these old mountain men who don't like people moving into what was once their wilderness."

"I'll go wake up your pard," said Luther. He picked up a large iron ring containing several keys. Whistling in a low tone, he disappeared through a doorway that led to the jail.

Slocum sat down in a battered wooden chair and acted as if he belonged there. He did not like the atmosphere of sheriff's offices or jails, somehow figuring he might never get outside again. The old Wanted posters from a couple of his past escapades still bothered him.

The sound of a key turning in a lock came from the jail section. Next came the creak of a heavy iron door swinging open.

"Sometimes Pawnee Joe gets a mite touchy when he gets woke up," said Frank. "But me and Luther know how to handle him. Take him outside and dunk his head in the horse trough. Works on most drunks. It gets their attention. Me 'n' my brother are big on getting folks' attention. You don't really get anywhere until you got them listening, really listening, to you. Once they listen, then you find most folks are meek as lambs."

A small wiry man dressed in buckskin came shambling out of the jail section. He paused for an instant in the doorway, eyes blinking against the daylight. He was not an old man, but his deeply lined face looked like a piece of tanned leather.

His dark, clouded eyes were deep-set beneath large, bushy salt-and-pepper eyebrows. His graying hair was worn back over his shoulders, tied in a knot like a pony's brush tail. His almost white beard was short, neatly trimmed by a barber in the past couple of days.

"This here is Pawnee Joe Miller," announced Luther Bannerman.

John Slocum stood up and started to extend his hand.

"Stay set," snapped the old man. His voice was high and crackling along the edges.

"How you feeling?" asked Frank Bannerman.

"Mouth tastes awful," answered the old man. "Tastes like somewhere between sour apple butter and buffalo shit."

The Bannerman brothers smiled broadly and Luther slapped the little man on the shoulder.

"You gotta think about quitting that stuff," said Luther.

"This morning is the time I'll agree." Pawnee Joe took a deep breath. "How'd I end up in jail?"

"We pulled you in when you threatened to kill two flatlanders."

Pawnee Joe asked, "What did they do to rile me up?'

The Bannerman boys shrugged.

"Reckon I can't remember." Pawnee Joe took another long breath.

He closed one eye and looked at John Slocum with a curious stare. "What makes you interested in me?"

"Sheriff Fillmore says you're going to be my partner."

"Ben always gets these wild hairs."

"We're supposed to find Horace Tremont's wife."

Pawnee Joe coughed, then asked, "She run off, eh?"

"Nobody knows for sure."

"Tremont's a fool. He don't know true love can't be bought. Either a woman gives it, natural-like, or she pretends."

Luther joined in. "Sheriff Fillmore thinks she may have been kidnapped."

"For ransom?" The little man belched.

"By some bunch of no-accounts riding through," added Frank. "We poked around and found this bunch of saddle tramps was in town for a couple of days. They're real trash. Rode in from the high plains over'n Kansas. We didn't know they were in town until the Tremont woman turned up missing."

The little man laughed. "That's like you Bannermans. Close the barn door after somebody steals the heifer. How's old Horace taking all this?"

"Not well," said Luther. "Which is why you two boys are going out after that bunch."

Pawnee Joe looked at Slocum with unblinking eyes. "You're supposed to be my partner?"

"That's what the high sheriff says," Slocum said.

"You know what you're about?"

"Maybe."

"Can you use that sixgun?"

"When I have to."

"You like using it?" The little man belched again.

"It's a tool. Handier'n some."

"Good enough answer," said Pawnee Joe, and he smiled at Slocum. "Being a good citizen is a fine and noble act. I done it a few times myself. Usually got paid with kind words and a sweet farewell. You been to see Horace Tremont about paying us?"

"He's made a good offer."

Pawnee Joe's eyes squinted to narrow slits. "How much?"

"A thousand for looking, ten thousand if we get her back."

The old man's mouth puckered and a wheezing sound came from his lips. The Bannerman brothers' mouths dropped open with astonishment.

The old mountain man laughed. "I ain't going unless we split it down the middle. Fair enough?"

"Can you handle yourself?" Slocum asked. "I don't want anything to do with a bottle baby with the shakes."

A deadly silence fell over the office.

The trapper's right hand came up to caress his beard. "Reckon you're from the flatlands," he said in a mild voice. "Folks around here know I just go on a toot after a long stretch back in the hills. Whatever comes up, you can depend on me to carry my share of the load."

Slocum asked, "When will you be ready to get started?"

"Right after I get some food in my belly." Pawnee Joe turned to the Bannerman brothers. "You got my guns and Bowie knife?"

Luther nodded and opened a drawer. "Right where you left them before you started prowling the saloons."

Pawnee Joe saw the surprised look on John Slocum's face. "I leave my weapons with these boys before starting out. That way I can't kill nobody if an argument starts. Ben Fillmore's idea, and it saves a lot of trouble." The little man chuckled as he took the weapons from Luther Bannerman.

Slocum looked at Frank Bannerman. "Who was this fellow who saw the woman pulled into an alley?' he asked.

"Ned Barton's his name."

"Is he reliable?'

"Likes a few whiskeys now and then, but he keeps to himself. Does a little gardening on the edge of town, raises a few horses, and minds his own business."

"Mind if we talk with him?"

Frank Bannerman looked thoughtful. "I'll draw you a map to find his place."

"And I'll grab a bite to eat, get us some supplies, and get ready to leave," said Pawnee Joe Miller.

Ned Barton's log cabin was a ramshackle structure built on a small knoll overlooking a brook on the south side of town. The logs were chinked with clay, the roof constructed from rough fir poles and large patches of sod.

A young man was weeding a large garden when John Slocum rode into the yard. The man stood up, removed a straw hat, and wiped the sweat from his forehead with a red bandana.

Slocum tied the reins of the chestnut Morgan to a gate-post and walked over to where the man was standing. They were surrounded by rows and mounds of earth, freshly plowed, with some green plants peeking out of the ground.

"Welcome," said Ned Barton, wiping his hand on the red bandana. "I get less visitors than I like out here."

Slocum introduced himself and explained the reason for his visit.

"I saw two men grab the woman," Ned Barton explained. "The whole thing took place maybe half a block from where I was standing. I was talking to a printer who works for the *Rocky Mountain News*. We'd been having a few beers and discussing the fate of the world."

"Did you see the woman's face?" Slocum asked.

"Hell no," said Barton jovially. "It didn't really register that strong with me. I figured it was a man and wife having a quarrel. I've been told married folks sometimes have disputes. Wouldn't know myself, because I've never had the pleasure of gettin' hitched."

"Did you get a good look at the men?"

"Tough-looking. The kind you wouldn't want standing behind you whether it was midnight or high noon."

"Did the printer see anything?"

"Nope. I suggested we walk down the alley. He thought I was making it up."

"What did you see in the alley?" Slocum wanted to know.

"Two men riding away. The woman was riding sidesaddle in front of one fellow."

Slocum asked, "Can you give me a description?"

"Of the woman? I didn't see her close up."

"What kind of horses were they riding?"

"That's easy enough," said Barton. "One horse was black with a white patch near the end of the tail. I didn't see the animal's face."

"And the other horse?"

"A nice golden-colored one. You could spot it a mile away."

"What about the men?"

"One was wearing dark clothes and other fellow had on one of those fancy Mexican coats. I don't know what they're called, but they have all that embroidery and gold stitching on them. That one also wore a big Mexican hat like you see sometimes when a bunch come up from Taos."

"You didn't report this to the sheriff?"

Ned Barton laughed easily. "Well, I've learned not to meddle in other people's business. You look like you've been out here for a while. You know what I'm talking about. Live and let live. Don't snoop into your neighbor's corral."

Slocum looked around the yard. "Nice place," he said.

"Keeps me busy keeping the weeds down and things in shape," said Ned Barton.

"How do you make a living?"

"I sell the vegetables from the garden." Ned Barton did not appear to be offended by the question. "See, I've been out here for almost three years. It didn't take long for me to realize that prospecting for silver was a risky business. Maybe you'll find something, maybe not. But every person digging for paydirt has to eat. I raise the vegetables, sell them in town to restaurants or to someone passing by. The soil is pretty good here and I got plenty of water from the creek. All in all, I'm a fairly happy man. Not getting rich, never going to make a big strike, but farming gives me time to think."

"Sounds like a good life," Slocum said.

"It beats knocking around in the hills or roaming across the plains."

"You have a point there."

"You aiming to track down that woman?"

"Sheriff Fillmore asked me to find her."

"That shouldn't take too much time," said Ned Barton.

"Why not?"

"Well, I come back from town and was out watering the garden," Barton explained. "Across the creek is the trail going down to Raton Pass and on down into Taos and Mexico. Those two men and their partners come riding along about sundown. That same woman was riding amongst them. She was on a mule."

Slocum felt like pounding Ned Barton on the head with a club. Instead, he asked, "How many were there in the party?"

"There was that same woman," answered Barton. "The same two men I saw in the alley. Riding the same horses. Plus, they was another woman in the bunch. Older woman, I'd judge, although the trail is a piece aways. And behind her was two more men."

"Four men and two women."

"Yep."

"Why didn't you mention this to the Bannerman brothers?"

Ned Barton looked surprised. "They never asked me. All they wanted to talk about was what happened in the alley. Should I have said something about it?"

Slocum was already moving toward the chestnut Morgan. "Next time, it might be a good idea," he said.

4

They stopped for the night in a valley fed by a small stream that flowed out of the snow-topped mountains. Pawnee Joe began to gather kindling for a fire, while John Slocum led the horses to the water, stood by while they drank, then hobbled the animals for the night. Not far away a huge towering rock shaped like a castle loomed above the landscape. Slocum came back to find Pawnee Joe humming to himself while bacon sizzled on an iron skillet. The aroma of sourdough biscuits made Slocum realize the extent of his hunger.

"She'll be ready in a minute," said Pawnee Joe, taking a stick and poking at the fire. "Bacon and biscuits ain't a bad meal considering we're moving so fast."

"You ever rode after men before?" Slocum asked.

Pawnee Joe jabbed the fire again with the stick. He hunkered back and chuckled. "Just a few times in my life," he said. "Mostly been a personal matter. Some galoot wanted my furs or a piece of my hide. A couple of Injuns thought about hanging my hair up on their lodgepoles. The first couple of times I went out of my way to avoid hurting those people. You ever do that?"

Slocum nodded. "Once or twice."

"Did it teach you anything?" asked the mountain man. His weathered face turned to Slocum with a questioning expression.

"I didn't stay around long enough to find out."

"You should have stayed. You'd have learned that wolves can seldom be tamed into lapdogs. Once a lobo, always a lobo. Maybe you can train a wolf to sit in your lap, but some night when you're not looking he'll sink his fangs into your balls! He'll be munching while you're wondering what came over your nice little pet. Nosiree! Someone crosses me, I shoot to kill. Never pull your gun unless you aim for the heart. Now"—and here the old man pulled a covered skillet out of the fire—"we better quit jawing and eat supper. Help yourself to some bacon and biscuits."

As they ate, and afterward, sitting around the embers of the campfire, Pawnee Joe Miller asked Slocum about his past. The little man listened as Slocum spoke of his life in Georgia before the War. Slocum remembered the happy time with his daddy during a trip to Savannah, where the young man stood on the bustling wharves of the South's busiest seaport.

Slocum remembered muscular, mahogany-skinned Negros loading bales of tobacco and cotton on tall-masted sailing ships. He listened to their melodic singing, a sorrowful refrain that offered little promise for an easier life.

Punctuating the music were heavy grunts as the slaves strained under the weight of heavy bales that were stacked on wooden pallets. Then came the creaky noise of the block and tackle as the cargo was raised into the air, then across the deck and dropped into the cargo hold.

Slocum told the mountain man about the excitement of that first day in a large city. "Hotheaded secession speechmakers were all over Savannah," Slocum recalled. "They were hollering about breaking away from the Union. Later, my daddy took me to the slave market where men and women were being bought and sold like animals. Slavery was a way of life in the South back then, but I felt something was wrong that afternoon."

Then, as the fire turned to ashes, Slocum mentioned his brother Robert's desire to return to their Georgia farm after the War. "We both planned to meet back home and build ourselves the finest farm in that part of the country," said Slocum.

"What happened to Robert?" Pawnee Joe asked.

"He didn't make it," Slocum said, his voice sad and husky.

Slocum fought under the command of a humorless Presbyterian artillery officer, Thomas Jackson. At Bull Run and Manassas, the thrill-seekers from Washington came out in their elegant carriages to view the battle as a thrilling spectacle, bringing their picnic baskets with them, champagne, roast chicken.

John Slocum explained that the Confederates held the line, that the Yankees were broken by the fury of Jackson's Brigade. The rebels laughed at the sight of Washington gentlemen racing their rigs through the Yankee retreat.

"We came across a Yankee general's wagon filled with wine to celebrate the victory," Slocum related. "I got my first taste of champagne beside a creek filled with dead bodies. I can still see that water turning pink with the blood of dead men."

After that, John Slocum became a "foot cavalryman," an infantryman in Jackson's amazing Valley campaign. They marched thirty, sometimes forty miles in a day, and fought like fresh soldiers upon arrival at their destination.

"That's where I learned to never give up," he explained. "Battles are won by men who keep going when their minds say quit."

There was splendor and turmoil as Jackson's soldiers rolled back through the Shenandoah Valley, under hot pursuit from Union armies. Waking hours were filled with smoke, dust, the tangy scent of burnt powder and death. Then Jackson took on the Yankees for a second round at Manassas. Many of the Confederate troops were half-starved, an army of ragged men without supplies or support. Slocum saw many men walk barefoot into battle.

"What kind of weapon did you use?" asked Pawnee Joe.

"I started out with a Brown Bess musket," Slocum answered. "She was accurate putting a minnie ball into a bluecoat at a fairly good distance. During the second scrap at Manassas I took a Spencer carbine off a dead Yankee sniper."

Slocum was promoted that day to corporal of a sharpshooters group. His men prowled the front lines seeking Yankee officers as their targets. Sniper duty was grim and ugly. Slocum did not like the killing, but he decided sharpshooting was a part of soldiering.

Many nights were spent shivering in cold rain, waiting for dawn to break over a Yankee encampment. Once the morning light came rising in the east, Slocum and his men zeroed in on Yankee officers. Once their targets were hit, they hightailed it back to safety.

Other times were spent slogging through cold spring mud, weighted down by the Spencer carbine and belts of ammunition. By now Slocum was a combat veteran who had learned to remain aloof from the other men. This distance was a way to avoid grief when someone died.

His brother, Robert, was a lieutenant when the battle of Gettysburg started. John Slocum was a sergeant in charge of the Confederate sharpshooters on Little Round Top.

Pickett's division charged through a peach orchard and Slocum's group laid down withering rifle fire against the attack. The blasts of rifles roared above the cries of wounded men. Slocum's men shot so fast they had to reload with rags wrapped around their hands to prevent blisters from glowing rifle barrels.

Slocum concentrated on Yankee officers, his prey. He kept firing at the gold braid of Yankee epaulets, killing men as Pickett's doomed division buckled under the heavy fire.

Robert Slocum was killed that day by a rifle shot from a Union soldier. John found his brother's body past sundown, stiff and cold, among the dead and wounded on a torchlit field. He knelt beside his brother's corpse and remained there for hours, praying for a future that could never become reality.

After Gettysburg, Slocum became more of a loner. He concentrated on his sharpshooting skills and was promoted to personal courier for General Robert E. Lee.

"After the War ended I drifted out here," Slocum said.

"Still drifting?" asked Pawnee Joe.

"I get cramped staying in one place."

"Know the feeling," said the mountain man. "I've lived with it since I headed up the Missouri on my first beaver-trapping expedition."

Slocum glanced up into the star-studded night sky. "Sorry about rambling on about the War," he told Pawnee Joe.

"Helps a man to talk about things," grunted the little man. "Well, I'm turning in."

Slocum stood up and opened his bedroll. "We better get an early start in the morning."

Pawnee Joe nodded. "I figure we'll catch up with that bunch sometime tomorrow evening. Sooner if they are still poking along."

They ate cold bacon and biscuits the next morning, broke camp as the first rays of sun were streaming in the east. They rode until almost noon, then stopped alongside a canyon and inspected the terrain. Pawnee Joe jumped down from his horse, checked hoofmarks on the trail, picked up a piece of horse manure in his hand.

"They're about six hours ahead of us," the little man said. "How do you reckon on handling them?"

"We can figure that out when we catch up," answered Slocum.

"They're not in a big hurry," said Pawnee Joe.

"We may be chasing a wild goose," Slocum pointed out. "Besides, they don't know we're on their tail."

"They will," laughed the little man, crawling back into the saddle.

He was silent for the next hour, staring off into the mountains. His leathery brow was furrowed with worry lines. It was one thing, Pawnee Joe thought, to track down a gang of bandits. It might take a miracle to come out of such an undertaking with Slocum, himself, and Mary Jo Tremont alive.

The canyon, several days' ride south of Denver, was as ancient as the Rocky Mountains. It held a secret history among the men who rode the outlaw trail in the West.

Formed in the side of a ravine so that entry was made only from a northerly angle, the entrance was hidden from the surrounding area by a large granite rock. Once a man had gone around the rock, the opening permitted single-file entry into a large bowl-shaped area. The canyon was a natural shelter from the weather and enemies. An outcropping of rock jutted over the western rim like a partial roof.

Primitive tribes inhabiting the land long before the Utes and Arapahoes appeared had camped in the canyon. Pieces of their sun-fired pottery could still be found scattered around on the ground. As these ancient tribes passed away, the Indians secured their wild mustangs within the high rock walls. The braves went out onto the plains, roped the wild ponies, and drove the powerful animals to the canyon to be broken for riding.

When white men moved into Jefferson Territory the canyon became a secluded hideout for men living outside the law. A group of *Comancheros,* traders and sometime bandits, camped in the canyons when the Santa Fe Trail was opened. From this haven they rode out onto the plains to raid wagon trains.

During their stay in the canyon, the *Comancheros* constructed several lean-to shacks around a pool of running water. When snow began to fall, the gang moved into four large caves in the red rimrock. The caves still contained furs left behind by the campers.

Through the years, word of the canyon passed along the outlaw grapevine. And, in time, the location of the sheltered canyon became known to the abductors of Mary Jo Tremont. It was normal for them to stay in the canyon whenever they were on the owlhoot trail.

The gang of four men and one woman were not thinking of the history of the canyon. They rode around the rock, entered the canyon, and dismounted. Their attention was directed toward their animals, which they stripped of their saddles and led to the pool for watering. The care of their animals was almost a ritual with the gang. They were not sentimental people who loved their horses. They kept the animals in good shape because a person on foot in the wilderness was clearly at peril.

Mary Jo Tremont sat astride a bay gelding, the mule having long since been pressed into service as a pack animal, while the bandits went on with their chores. She had learned to remain quiet, not draw attention to herself. Although she had led a sheltered life, first in Chicago, later in Denver as Horace Tremont's wife, Mary Jo knew the gang could be brutal.

Mary Jo had remained quiet about her marital status and the wealth of her husband. She had deliberated on the matter and decided silence was her best course. She had been snatched into an alley, thrown aboard a horse as two men rode away. She had been unable to cry out because the Mexican, the stinking one, kept his hand clasped firmly over her mouth.

The woman with the gang, a hard-looker named Mattie, had tried to become friendly with Mary Jo. The kidnapped girl eyed the forty-one-year-old woman with suspicion. Mary Jo responded to Mattie's questions with brief answers.

Mattie rode beside Mary Jo during the day. The older woman was a chatterbox, rattling on about her luckless life. She spoke of the treachery of men, how she should have stayed in the whorehouse in Texas and not rode off with Frank Wylie, the leader of the gang.

Frank Wylie was a loser, an outlaw who could seldom gather enough loot to provide food for himself and the gang. He was unschooled, lacked discipline, and was anonymous enough to be wanted under several different names.

Mattie left her horse drinking at the pool. She came over and looked up at Mary Jo sitting astride the bay gelding.

She said,"I think these fools would leave you up there all night. They're so dumb I don't see how they make a dollar."

Frank Wylie came shambling over. He was a dark-haired man whose muscle was gradually turning to flab. A roll of fat hung over his belt.

"You're sure a pretty thing," Wylie said.

"Don't listen to him," Mattie said. "I was struck by his sweet talk and look where it got me."

"I ought to shoot you and keep this lady," said Frank Wylie, sucking in his stomach.

"Help her down," said Mattie.

Frank Wylie raised his arms and helped Mary Jo Tremont off the horse. *My, my,* he thought, *you are just about the most beautiful woman I've ever seen. Too bad I had to meet you when this old whore has her brand on my hide.*

"Thank you," Mary Jo said. She held out her wrists. They were bound by a rawhide thong. "Can you untie me for the time we're here?"

Frank Wylie looked thoughtful. "Well, you ain't gonna run far, lady," he said curtly.

"Untie her," Mattie snapped. "I can use some help cooking dinner."

"All right," Frank Wylie growled. He tried to untie the rawhide. "Dang thing is all knotted up."

"Cut it," said Mattie.

"We'll need to tie her tomorrow."

"Like you said, she ain't running away."

"You never know what a woman will do," Frank grumbled.

"Where's she going to run to?"

"Hell, I don't know."

Frank pulled a knife from a sheath behind his neck. It had a long, thin blade "My Arkansas toothpick," he said.

"You want something to eat?" Mattie said in a grating tone.

"I expect so." Irritation edged Frank Wylie's tone.

"Then untie her and we'll start fixing supper."

Frank cut the rawhide thong.

"Thank you," said Mary Jo.

"Sure." Frank started to say something and saw Mattie's glaring stare. He bit down on his lower lip and walked off toward the pool of water. The other members of the gang were standing there.

"Can you cook?" Mattie asked.

Mary Jo Tremont twisted her hands around her wrists, getting the blood to circulate again. "I can cook some," she answered.

"Well, all we got is a slab of salt pork and pinto beans," Mattie confided. "Course, you know that. You been eating with us the last few days. Help me pick up some sticks and we'll start a fire."

As the woman walked across the canyon floor, Mary Jo Tremont asked, "Where are they taking me?"

"Down south."

"What do they plan on doing with me?"

"It ain't a bad deal," Mattie said. She bent and pulled up a tuft of dried grass. "We're taking you to Mexico. Frank knows a man down there who pays a good price for fair-haired women."

"*Sell* me?" Mary Jo Tremont's voice was tinged with fear.

"It ain't as bad as you think," Mattie explained. "You'll be sold to some rich man who likes blond women. A good looker like you will fetch a real high price. And any man who pays a big price for a woman is going to treat her right. Likely you'll have some of those Mexican women who'll do the work. All you'll have to do is lay around and keep your owner happy."

Mary Jo Tremont wondered about a woman who would consider slavery to be a good position in life. Then a rigid notion formed in her mind. "I won't allow myself to be sold."

"Dearie, you don't have anything to say about it."

"There are laws."

"Pshaw," said Mattie. "Don't give this bunch any trouble. I've seen them kill. You start acting up and they'll pass you around for pleasuring. They'd have done it by now if I wasn't along to make them mind their manners. When men get to deciding twixt money and woman pleasure, most times money takes second place."

Mary Jo shuddered at the thought of being manhandled, perhaps raped, by these rough, uncouth men. Frank Wylie was a youngish man, fairly good-looking, but crude in his mannerisms. The other three gang members were filthy in habit, appearance, and thought. Two were Mexicans; the third was a tobacco-chewing old man who rode a stolen mule. They eyed her throughout the day, often casting leering stares in her direction. She knew what notions were racing through their minds.

Mattie said, "We'd better quit jabbering and get supper. Frank gets downright put out whenever he gets hungry."

"Don't you ever get tired of this kind of life?" asked Mary Jo.

"Tired? I hate it." Mattie eyes flashed with anger. "But I don't have a choice in the matter. I come into this vale of tears without nothing and, when I leave, I expect things'll be the same way, dearie."

"You could get a job."

"I got no education. I can't read, can't write, and no-body ever taught me ciphering. The only thing I got to sell is my body and, lately, Frank has been complaining be-cause I'm getting a little shopworn. I expect we'll make a pretty penny when you're sold. I get a share just like everyone else. We ain't had much luck since I come with Frank. Pickings have been mighty slender. Stagecoaches all got a shotgun guard these days. People travel in cara-vans across the plains and every time we stop at a house the people come out with a shotgun in their hands. Living like this ain't easy."

"You could be a maid," Mary Jo said.

"I wouldn't know how to act around folks who could afford a maid."

"Well, you could do something else. Help me escape and I'll give you some money to live on."

Mattie's eyes took on a hooded look. "Where would you get money?"

"My husband would pay to get me back."

"You didn't say you were married."

"He'd pay a lot."

Mattie said, "How much money?"

"Double what you'd get if I was sold."

"How would you know how much that was?"

"You probably have an idea," said Mary Jo.

"Frank said it might be a thousand dollars." Mattie spoke as if such a sum was beyond reality.

"Help me get back to Denver," said Mary Jo. "My hus-band would pay that and more to get me back."

"Let me think about it."

"Let me know as soon as possible."

"We'd best get started with the cooking," said Mattie. She picked up a pile of sticks and went moving off to where the men stood around the pool of water.

Mary Jo Tremont followed the older woman. She was conscious of the men looking at her, wondered if she could somehow use their interest to an advantage. She decided against doing anything that might rile up their tempers. Instead, she would concentrate on Mattie's greed.

5

John Slocum and Pawnee Joe Miller hobbled their horses
and left them in a grove of trees. They checked the ammunition in their pistols, made sure their repeating rifles were
loaded. Silently they walked to the rock wall surrounding
the canyon.

They crawled carefully up the slanting, rock-strewn
slope. They wanted to avoid making a sound that would
alert the gang. Nearing the top, they removed their hats
and peered over the rimrock.

The outlaws were scattered around the canyon floor. A
tall, paunchy Mexican man in a Chihuahua hat and an ornate coat strolled near the entrance to a cave. Two men
were talking beside a pool of water, while a third man was
stretched out on the ground using his saddle as a pillow. A
young woman was resting on a blanket while an older
woman was stirring a pot of food over a campfire.

Slocum also noticed that one horse in the group was

black with a white tail, just as Ned Barton had described.
Another animal was a golden palomino color.

"I'll take the two by the pool," said Slocum. He pulled
his Sharps repeating rifle into firing position.

Pawnee Joe Miller licked his lips, wet his finger, and
tested the wind.

"You don't want to talk with them?" he asked in a whisper.

Slocum shook his head. "The time for talking is past.
That would just give them the time to use Mrs. Tremont as
a shield." His voice was low. "Get ready. We'll shoot on
the count of three."

Slocum sighted on the chest of the old man by the pool.
It was no different, he told himself, than shooting a Yankee
officer. Trying to talk with men who kidnapped a woman
was foolish. It would be as futile as trying to talk with a
scorpion. He held the rifle with a steady hand, resting the
barrel on the level rimrock. He focused on the unkempt
beard that hung down from the old man's chin.

"I'm ready," whispered Pawnee Joe.

"One . . . two . . . three."

Slocum squeezed the trigger. Orange flame spurted
from the barrel of his rifle.

He heard the explosion of Pawnee Joe's rifle.

Down below, it was as if a rope had been flung around
the old man's chest, pulling him back and down. His arms
flew wildly up in the air and his mouth opened wide. He
was knocked off his feet and went splashing back into the
pool of water.

At the same time, Pawnee Joe's bullet hit the stomach
of the Mexican with the big hat. He screamed, yelled in
Spanish, and crumpled to the ground.

Instantly, Slocum swung his rifle around and aimed at
his second target. The man looked frightened. His mouth

was wide open. His eyes were staring at the corpse of the old man in the water. His hand was speeding for his holstered pistol when Slocum's bullet smashed into his brain.

The power of the slug buckled his body. He fell forward on his face as the lower part of his body was knocked backward.

Pawnee Joe's rifle cracked. The bullet hit the body of the outlaw who was resting with his head on the saddle. His belly bucked up under the impact of the bullet. His chest arced high, then slammed back against the ground.

Pawnee Joe asked, "You want to make sure they're dead?"

"I don't feel like trying to get them to a doctor," Slocum responded.

Down below, the Mexican with the big hat started to stand up. His hands were red with his own blood. Pawnee Joe took aim slightly above the outlaw's red-frothed mouth. He pulled the trigger and the man was knocked back against the rocks.

The middle-aged woman was screaming. She dropped her ladle beside the campfire, spun around, and started running wildly around the canyon floor.

"You wanna kill her?" asked Pawnee Joe. The end of his rifle barrel followed the woman's figure.

"Naw, I don't like shooting women." Slocum stood up and looked down into the canyon.

"Suit yourself."

"I'm going down and get Mrs. Tremont."

Pawnee Joe nodded. "I'll cover you and her."

His rifle was sighted on the older woman, who was now bending over one of the dead men. She was screaming, a high-pitched wail that resounded off the stone walls of the canyon.

Pawnee Joe Miller lay on the rimrock and looked down

into the canyon. The four bodies were sprawled down below, unmoving, with flies starting to buzz around the corpses. For a long time after John Slocum went down the slope, Pawnee Joe Miller just sat and looked down through the gathering gloom.

I don't like killing, he thought. Death had walked by his side since his first trip up the Missouri River into the wilderness. He had killed, animal and man, until the finality of the act had been blotted from his mind. In all of the years since he had killed his first man, he had moved through the wilderness spilling blood.

Now it was past time to hang up his guns. He didn't want to kill any more, whether the target be a good or bad man. It didn't matter whether human or animal, enough blood had been spilled. Killing was an act of judgment, a matter best handled between a man and his Maker.

John Slocum introduced himself to Mary Jo Tremont. Her long blond hair was covered by the cowl of her woolen cloak, her white skin contrasting dramatically against the dark fabric. Her face was smudged with dirt, but the clearness of her complexion was still evident.

Although the young woman had been frightened by the killings, there was a determined tilt to her chin. Her lips, full and red, were inviting to any man. Slocum looked closely into her eyes. They were deep, shimmering pools of light green.

John asked, "Did they hurt you?"

"I'm all right." Her voice was soft, controlled.

She looked away from his eyes.

John motioned his head toward the older woman, who was sobbing over the body of Frank Wylie. "What about her? Is she one of the gang?"

"That man was her lover," Mary Jo answered.

Slocum waved to Pawnee Joe, who held his position on the rimrock. "Come on down!" Slocum shouted.

Pawnee Joe answered by waving his Sharps repeating rifle. Then his head vanished from view.

"Who's that?" asked Mary Jo. "I thought you were alone."

"My partner." Slocum told her about the little mountain man.

His attention was drawn to the woman named Mattie. She was slumped over the corpse of Frank Wylie. Her anguished cries echoed off the canyon walls.

"She's harmless," said Mary Jo Tremont.

Slocum shook his head. "Not while guns are still on the corpses. I promised your husband and Sheriff Fillmore to get you back unharmed."

"Mattie is just confused."

"I'll get their guns," said Slocum.

Mattie clung to Frank Wylie's body as Slocum unbuckled the gunbelt, frisked the corpse for a hideout gun.

"You bastard!" Mattie spat. "You're a cold-blooded killer. You didn't give them a chance."

"Lady, kidnapping is not a game."

"You shot them without warning," said Mattie. Her face took on a dark, twisted expression. "I'll see you remember Frank Wylie until your dying day."

Slocum dismissed the threat. He asked, "Was that his name . . . Frank Wylie?"

Mattie's eyes glinted with hate. "We were talking about getting a little place in Texas."

"He grabbed the wrong woman," said Slocum. "He found himself a little place here in these mountains."

Mattie looked confused. "What are you talking about?"

"Frank found himself a grave," said Slocum.

"He was my man. The only love I ever had." Mattie sniffed.

"What's your name?" Slocum asked.

"Mattie. Mattie Pitzen."

"Well, Mattie, you've been riding with a dangerous bunch," Slocum told her. "Mrs. Tremont was kidnapped. I reckon the sheriff in Denver can decide what to do with you. You're welcome to ride back with us. I just don't want any trouble from you. I don't like troublesome women."

Mattie looked thoughtful. She crossed her heart with a blood-smeared finger. "I'll behave," she promised.

"Start by collecting all of their guns and belts," Slocum said. "You can keep any money you find on them."

Mattie snorted. "Wasn't a penny 'mong the whole bunch. That's why they decided to grab that woman in Denver. She woulda brought money down in Mexico. Frank had bad luck. Just like I've always had. Nothing ever worked out for me."

"It doesn't always have to be that way."

She smiled crookedly. "Aw, hell, I know what the future holds for me. A bed in a whorehouse, less and less customers as I get older, and death from the pox."

"Jesus, Mattie, you know how to make a man feel good."

"I know. Myself, I been knocked from pillar to post since I was knee-high to a gnat. Never had a chance in this damned world. All these stinking holier-than-thou respectable people looking down their noses at me. Lord, I'd like to cram crap down their throats with a shovel."

"Save that for later," Slocum advised. "Right now we got to get these bodies in the ground, else we'll have a mess in the morning. Any of this bunch happen to have a shovel?"

"Nope."

Slocum frowned. "Neither do I."

Mattie pointed to the canyon's rock wall. "We can put 'em in there."

Slocum followed the direction of her grimy finger. He saw the entrance to one of the canyon's caves.

"And we can close up the entrance with rocks," he said. "That'll keep out the wild animals."

After the bodies were placed in the caves and the entrance sealed with rocks, they rode away. Pawnee Joe had suggested that they camp outside the rocky canyon of death. The sun was falling behind the mountains as they rounded the large rock and headed up the trail to Denver. That night a camp was made beside a small stream. After a quick meal, they sank into their bedrolls and slept.

Slocum awoke during the night. He rose to a sitting position and glanced around the campsite. The fire had burned down to embers. The moon, a silver orb in a velvet black sky, silhouetted a figure standing on a knoll.

He looked over, saw that Mattie Pitzen and Pawnee Joe Miller were sleeping on opposite sides of the fire. The dark, slim figure in the moonlight had to be Mary Jo Tremont.

Slocum pulled on his boots, stood up, and carefully left the camp.

He did not want to startle the woman. He stopped a few yards from where she was standing. Clearing his throat with a low cough, he waited for her to respond.

She turned around.

"Is that you, Slocum?"

"Yes. Can't you sleep?"

"I keep thinking about the shooting."

He walked up and stood beside her. The silvery moonlight added to her beauty. He forced himself to avert his gaze from her face. She was incredibly beautiful, a young woman with cameo perfection. Her flawless features held a lustrous beauty that could shatter a man's heart. Every part of him longed to take her in his arms, to hold her in his embrace and talk to her about things that a man kept bottled up.

"I couldn't sleep," she said. "I would doze off and then I'd start to have a nightmare. All that shooting . . . how it started without any warning . . . I keep seeing those men going down. Kept seeing the blood spurting out of their bodies."

"That was the only way we could take them," Slocum said. "If they had been warned—well, you would have been their shield."

"Lord, I'm not placing blame on you. It is just . . . I've never seen anyone die before."

"How old are you?"

"Twenty-four."

He was astonished. "And you've never seen anyone die?"

"Not until today. I've been lucky, I guess." She gazed into his face. "How many men have you killed, Slocum?"

"Too many."

Standing there in the moonlight, she raised her face and brushed her lips against his mouth.

"I'm grateful for your help," she said warmly.

He started to put his arms around her, but she stepped away with a quickness that startled him.

"Mary Jo—"

"Sorry if I misled you," she said, keeping distance between them. "I'm married to Horace Tremont. I don't intend to commit adultery."

Slocum wondered if she was a teaser. He had known women who led men on, then delighted in evading their amorous advances.

Slocum looked glumly toward the young woman. "If you didn't plan on anything, why did you kiss me?"

"I was impulsive."

Suddenly, she kissed him again. Her warm lips pressed firmly against his mouth, her tongue a fiery dart that moved with a slow circular motion.

Slipping her hand down his body, she undid the buttons on his pants. Then, her hand slipped gently inside and her fingers encircled his throbbing flesh. He stiffened instantly as she began to stroke with a hard and rapid motion.

She pulled her lips away from his mouth. "I promised Horace I would never have intercourse with another man," she said huskily.

Suddenly, unexpectedly, she dropped to her knees before him. The moist fullness of her open lips was illuminated by the silver shafts of moonlight. Her mouth and lips moved over his firmness in a slow, tantalizing motion. He began to throb as the intensity of her pressure increased, as she drew him deep inside that warm and moist mouth.

Slocum stood there, feeling the fabulous sensations move through his body like warm, crashing waves. When it was over, she buttoned his trousers and stood up. "Horace always likes that," she said.

"Horace is a lucky man." Slocum spoke with sincerity.

"I think sleep will come a little easier now," Mary Jo said. "Besides, we'd better get back before the others miss us."

"Don't worry. They're sleeping soundly."

Slocum wanted to remain forever out in the moonlight with this beautiful woman.

Mary Jo giggled. "Don't get greedy, Slocum. That was just to show my appreciation for rescuing me. Now, I also promise you that when we get back to Denver I'll throw a great party for you. Horace loves parties. They give him a chance to let loose, get drunk, and forget that he is a silver king and richer than King Midas ever dreamed."

"What kind of party?" Slocum wondered if the festivities might include a repeat performance of this night's antics.

"A party to celebrate life."

"That sounds good."

"It will be," said Mary Jo, taking his arm and heading back to their campsite. "You will meet the wildest bunch of men that ever trod God's earth. Those are the miners who are friends of my husband. They're more than a bit crude, don't have very good table manners. They've been known to use an occasional off-color word during their conversations. But, overall, the prospectors are not a bad bunch of men. True, they're obsessed with finding sudden riches, and a few of them do. My Horace is a fine example of how fate can deal a winning hand."

"Why did you marry an old man like Horace?" Slocum asked.

"We have an understanding."

"Which is?"

"I come from a family with great breeding," answered Mary Jo. "My family tree goes back to the landing of the Pilgrims in Massachusetts. Unfortunately, breeding is about all they are capable of doing. They can't seem to hold jobs, always fail at business, and have the anemic blood of people who can't cope with things. I was expected to marry rich."

"You certainly did."

"Meeting Horace was an accident," she went on. "But we struck a bargain. I'll be his wife until he dies, then the Tremont fortune goes to me as his widow. Horace is failing in many ways. His mind isn't as sharp as it could be. He has several physical ailments. I'm his sweet young wife and, believe it or not, I am genuinely fond of him. He gets what you got whenever he feels the urge. I get kept in splendor, and my future is secure."

"Somehow that tells me there is a cynical hardness on your part."

Mary Jo chuckled. "Slocum, you will never understand women. We're all hard and cynical about men. Women start learning how to flirt when they are babies. They never stop using their wiles to get what they want from men. Occasionally you'll find a couple of women who are friends, but we are mostly loners. Like a wildcat or panther that prowls in these mountains. They don't hunt in pairs and neither do women. I'm just a little more honest than most women. Some women would claim to have married Horace for love. That's nonsense. Horace gets a young wife for his amusement in his old age because he can afford it."

Mattie Pitzen pretended to be asleep when Slocum and Mary Jo came back to camp. Mattie lay in her bedroll, her mind busy, and looked out into the moonlit darkness. She saw the couple come back to camp, holding hands. They were so young that a part of her wanted to cry for her lost youth and innocence.

She thought of Frank Wylie, who had once been crazy

about her. Crazy enough to catch Mattie's attention and cause her to ride off with him. Her thoughts brightened for a moment as she thought of Frank's lies about who he was, what he did for a living. He was not a West Texas rancher, just a plain out-of-work, out-of-money cowboy trying to pick up money on the owlhoot trail. Then she saw Frank's body lying on the ground of the canyon, blood spurting, a pink froth bubbling out of his mouth.

She lay her head back on the pillow as Slocum and Mary Jo walked to their bedrolls. People who judged and killed had to be given their due. Women who acted so high and mighty should be brought down a notch.

A dark little beast formed in her mind. Revenge began to occupy her thoughts. The beast smiled contentedly.

6

Horace Tremont sat behind a large, highly polished desk before a double window with the drapes drawn to shield him from a bright mid-afternoon sun. His offices were on the second floor of an office building purchased by his silver company. The building was one of the many enterprises purchased by Tremont after his lucky strike.

Tremont was listening to a report by his male secretary, who was reading figures that told of the silver miner's wealth.

Both men looked up when Luther and Frank Bannerman walked into the office without knocking. A wide grin spread across the deputy's face.

"We got some good news," said Frank.

"Yesiree!" Luther chortled. "Rider came hightailing it in from the south. Said John Slocum and your wife are riding this way."

"Thank God," said Tremont. He leaped out of his chair and started a little jigging dance.

"Look at that man," said Frank.

"A hot time in Denver tonight, I reckon," said Luther.

Horace Tremont stopped jigging around the office. "When will they get here?"

"Maybe a half-hour."

Tremont's face brightened.

"A band," he said, waving his thin arms at the male secretary. "Go see Elmer Johnson down at the hardware store. I want the Denver drum and bugle corps playing when Mary Jo gets to town. Just tell Elmer I'll buy new uniforms for the band if they'll play. He'll understand and get everyone together."

The secretary started out the office door. He paused and looked back at Tremont. "Where is the band supposed to set up?"

"In front of the sheriff's office," snapped Luther Bannerman.

"Spread the news," cried Tremont. "I want people cheering when my wife gets into town."

"Me 'n' Luther will tell the barkeeps," said Frank.

"Tell the saloonkeepers to buy a round for their customers, then close down. I want everyone out to welcome Mary Jo," said Tremont, looking impatiently for his hat.

"Close the saloons?" Luther looked doubtful.

"Just till my wife gets here," said Tremont. "Then I'll buy drinks for the rest of the night. The party is on Horace Tremont."

The Bannerman brothers moved out to spread the news.

Twelve hundred screaming, joyous people were gathered in front of the sheriff's office. Men, women, children— and probably a hundred dogs—were crowded into the street. Men laughed loudly, made sure they went over and clapped Horace Tremont on the back.

Tremont was genuinely liked by most people. The millions of dollars from his silver mine had not changed the man. He could be depended on for a grubstake, just as men had grubstaked Tremont before his bonanza days. Yet he was a pushover for hucksters and ne'er-do-wells.

Bottles of whiskey were passed from man to man. A liquor dealer had heard of Tremont's offer. He pulled a wagonload of bottles to the edge of the crowd. Four men were up in the wagon handing the bottles to outstretched hands.

The women were segregated into separate groups. The wives, mothers, and God-fearing widows were on one side of the street. They chatted in sedate tones and kept watchful eyes on the children.

They viewed the guzzling whiskey drinkers with evident distaste. Occasionally a wife would catch sight of her husband in the crowd. She would leave the other women and go to pull her mate away from the drinkers. When a sheepish man was led away by his wife, the onlookers crowed, jeered, and applauded with good humor.

Another group of women waited on the opposite side of the street. They were dressed in satin frocks, silk dresses, and low-cut gowns. These were the saloon girls, soiled doves, and women of the evening—Denver's painted ladies. A few were irritated by the event, but most were elated by the spontaneous celebration.

Now the drum and bugle corps blared out a melodic tune. People began to tap their feet to the beat of the music. Elmer Johnson, decked out in a red-and-white-striped coat, led the musicians with a baton.

Denver was ready for the return of John Slocum and Mary Jo Tremont.

When Slocum came riding through the streets, hearing the noise becoming louder, he looked over at Pawnee Joe Miller.

"What do you think that is?" he asked.

"Maybe a Fourth of July celebration," answered the little man.

"Except this isn't the right month."

Mary Jo Tremont said, "You never know in Denver. People can get excited about most anything."

Mattie Pitzen rode alongside the others. She was awed by the size of the growing frontier community. Her amazement kept her from commenting on the strange noise that seemed to be coming from around the corner.

Suddenly a man crossing an intersection caught a glimpse of Slocum's party.

"They're a-coming!" he whooped.

The crowd cheered.

Half a dozen men fired their pistols up into the sky.

The Denver drum and bugle corps tooted loudly.

Sheriff Ben Fillmore yelled that the next idiot to fire a pistol would be arrested.

A stout youth tossed a Chinese firecracker into the street.

Several horses neighed. The two mules pulling the whiskey wagon reared back, then tore into a wild run. The runaway team pulled the wagon across the sidewalk. They crossed a weed-covered vacant lot with a dozen yelping dogs in rapid pursuit.

The Bannerman brothers smiled and dug their elbows into each other's rib cages.

"A real shindig," said Luther.

Frank Bannerman couldn't hear what his brother was saying. Frank looked around, saw the turmoil, and shook his head in agreement. It was enjoyable to watch people having fun.

Warily, with his rifle resting across his saddle, Slocum led his group around the corner.

The crowd let loose with a giant, roaring sound of greeting. Men whooped, women cried, children screamed, and dogs barked. While drums rolled and horns blared, the gathering verged on the edge of hysteria. At any instant the crowd could become transformed into a mob.

Then a short, pudgy, benevolent-looking man in a black suit motioned for the band to stop playing. He stepped up on a bench in front of the sheriff's office, eyeing the crowd through square silver-rimmed spectacles.

Some of the people in the crowd recognized Reverend James Arlington, the Methodist minister. They began to hush the crowd while the Methodist ladies demanded respect for the preacher.

In a minute, the crowd had quieted so the preacher could speak. His deep voice had a calming effect. "Ladies and gentlemen, I suggest we bow our heads in thankful prayer for the safe return of Mrs. Mary Jo Tremont to our beautiful city."

A couple of whiskey-bent men started to object, then looked around and saw Sheriff Ben Fillmore's hooded eyes staring at them. They shut up and lowered their heads. The minister led the gathering in a long, poetic prayer.

They cheered when Horace and Mary Jo Tremont met before the sheriff's office. But now the mood of the crowd was subdued and the event was under the direction of Reverend Arlington. Another prayer was given by the preacher. Part of the crowd began to drift away.

Sheriff Fillmore ordered the preacher to keep calling for prayer.

"Come inside my office," the sheriff told Slocum. "I want to know what happened."

The two men sat across from each other at Sheriff Fillmore's desk. The lawman dipped into a desk drawer and pulled out two cigars. He handed one of the cigars to Slocum, then held out a match.

"The lady looks none the worse for wear," said Sheriff Fillmore, puffing his cigar to life. He blew smoke into the air.

Slocum recited the events of the rescue.

"You brought the woman back?" asked Fillmore.

Slocum looked dumbfounded.

"That Mattie woman, I mean."

"I didn't feel right doing anything else."

"I know what you mean," said Fillmore. "But you should have sent her south. What am I supposed to do with her?"

"Charge her with something?"

"Hell, the local government doesn't like paying to keep people in jail."

"She's your problem now," Slocum said.

Fillmore studied the ashen tip of his cigar. "Maybe I can give her to the U.S. marshal. That's the thing to do. Mattie can become the marshal's problem. He'll want to get involved in this affair."

"We rescued Mrs. Tremont. What else needs to be done?"

"The marshal likes to send a report to Washington."

"He can be my guest."

"He is also a glory seeker."

"Let him take the credit."

Fillmore laughed. "All you want is the cash?"

"Naturally, I expect to be paid. Pawnee Joe and I did what we set out to do."

"Don't worry. Tremont always makes good on his promises."

"I never doubted that. What do you want us to do with Mattie Pitzen?"

"I just explained. Give her to the U.S. marshal."

"Where is his office?"

"Tom is over at Georgetown." Fillmore went into a lengthy explanation of the law and order problems in the new mining town.

When he finished, Slocum said, "Pawnee Joe is outside watching the Pitzen woman. I don't expect he'll want to stand there until the marshal gets back to Denver."

Sheriff Ben Fillmore took another puff on his cigar. "I don't want her in my jail. No facilities for women. Dang, Slocum, you should have shot her or turned her head south. They surely got need of whores down in Taos or wherever she would have gone."

"I did what I thought was best."

"No complaint," said Fillmore quickly. "She just presents a little bit of a problem. Look, I'll take her and have the Bannerman boys get a room for her over the Paradise Saloon. I'm not filing charges. She can hang around there, maybe earning her keep, until Tom Jackson gets back from Georgetown."

"Jackson's the U.S. marshal?"

"Mister Guts and Glory himself," said Fillmore. "Fancies himself as the best lawman in the West. And he isn't a bad peacemaker. Well"—Fillmore shrugged his shoulders —"I never liked men who keep their clothes a little too clean, their gunbelts too fancy, their guns all polished and oiled like a museum piece. They get a little too fussy, overly fancy, and too quick to draw on another man. Put a tin star on their chest and you get someone like Tom Jackson."

* * *

Slocum left the sheriff's office. Outside the crowd had dispersed and only a few diehards still hung around. Among them was a man from the *Rocky Mountain News*, who was taking notes while Pawnee Joe Miller answered the reporter's questions.

"You're Mr. Slocum?" asked the reporter. He introduced himself and said his name was Charles Winters. "We're planning on giving this story our best effort. Pawnee Joe says you're from Calhoun County, Georgia?"

Slocum nodded.

"Were you afraid of the Wylie gang?"

Slocum nodded again. "A smart man is always afraid."

"Is that why the two of you ambushed the gang?"

Slocum's face went taut. "It wasn't an ambush."

Pawnee Joe added, "I've been trying to explain that to this jasper, Slocum. He keeps wanting to say we ambushed that bunch of trash."

Charles Winters grinned quickly. "Merely a figure of speech. My story will be playing up the heroic aspects of the rescue of Mary Jo Tremont from the infamous Wylie bandit gang."

"Infamous?" repeated Slocum.

"Maybe notorious is a better word," said the reporter. "You'll agree they were a dastardly band of desperadoes."

"Dumb desperadoes," answered Slocum.

Sheriff Fillmore came out of his office. He greeted the reporter, then spoke in a calming tone to Mattie Pitzen. He explained to the woman that she would be staying at the Paradise Saloon. Mattie looked fearful at first, but the sheriff's sedate voice and easy manner eased her mind.

"I need to talk with the lady for a few additional quotes," said Charles Winters.

Fillmore took the woman's arm. "She'll be at the Paradise."

"I'll walk along with you," Slocum said. "What about you, Pawnee?"

"I'm going to stay and talk with this gent," said the little mountain man. "It ain't very often I get to answer questions like a hero."

"Enjoy it," said Slocum. He started to walk away.

"But I'll need information from you," protested Charles Winters.

"Pawnee Joe speaks for me," Slocum said over his shoulder.

Things were happening as Slocum walked down the street and turned onto Larimer. He had never seen a town so lively. The saloons were open again, the bars crowded, as drinkers took advantage of the free drinks being paid for by Horace Tremont. Every table in the Paradise Saloon was taken; there was scarcely room to squeeze past drinkers at the bar.

Across the way, the Denver Social Club was filled with a clamorous group of drinkers. The bartenders rushed to keep their glasses filled. Whoops and hollers came pouring out of the Western Brewing Company next door. Even the Bucket of Blood, a den of hardcases, horse thieves, and ne'er-do-wells, was filled with happy sounds.

Slocum stopped and stood on a corner, smiling. He wished a woman was available to share his sense of well being. Mary Jo Tremont was back with her husband; Elizabeth Winston was undoubtedly with her family back East.

While he stood there, half a dozen men came bursting out of the Bucket of Blood. They linked arms and staggered out into the street. Their voices were raised in song.

One man staggered, went down into the street, and fell to his knees. He pawed the earth and raised his face to the darkening sky. He howled like a lobo wolf.

The man's companions gathered round to witness his struggle to stand up. With a wild bellow, the man rose and weaved unsteadily on his shaky legs.

"Ladies and gents," he roared. "We are gathered tonight in the sight of the Almighty to drink whiskey furnished by Horace Tremont. Mister Strike-It-Rich hisself has seen fit to provide liquid refreshments for the people of Denver whilst he welcomes back the wife of his dreams. I say—"

After that introduction the drunk preached a sermon asking for the Almighty to supply every man with a woman like Mary Jo Tremont. If such women could not be found on this earth, then the Almighty should have the price of whores lowered to a reasonable figure.

As the man slurred through the words of his speech, his friends shouted, yelled their amens, and clapped their hands. The noise brought other men pouring out of the saloons. The intersection was soon filled with shouting men.

A newcomer yelled out that the man needed a text, some reference point for his sermon. The drunk said the sons of bitches in his congregation would not know a Bible if they were pounded on the head with the Good Book.

This startled someone in the group, who decided the mock sermonizer was besmirching God's name. Someone threw a punch and a fight started. Everyone got involved punching, kicking, pushing, and yelling like crazed panthers.

Then a man was punched in the side. He fell back into a large mound of horse manure. That caused everyone to start laughing. Men who had been fighting a moment before were now standing with their arms around each other's shoulders. They laughed at the man trying to clean the manure off his trousers, started singing again, and moved off into the saloons. The mock preacher and the man with manure on his pants linked arms, talked about eternal friendship, and vanished through the batwing doors of a saloon.

Slocum smiled, shook his head, and walked up the street to the Paradise Saloon. He felt like a stranger in an alien land, a man without a home and without purpose.

7

Mary Jo Tremont kept her word. Two days after her return
to Denver, the Tremont mansion was the site of a party to
honor John Slocum and Pawnee Joe Miller. A couple of
hundred people were invited to the celebration, which was
held on the grounds of the Tremont mansion. By six
o'clock that evening the guests had gathered at the back of
the mansion.

Horace Tremont had erected four barbecue pits and
hired a band of Mexican musicians. Every available car-
penter in Denver had been hired to build a dance floor for
the party.

The cook hired for the occasion rang a dinner bell to
signal that the food was ready to serve. Two hogs and a
young steer had been cooking over an open fire most of the
day. In addition to those barbecued meats, an iced barrel of

oysters sat at the beginning of the food line.

John Slocum left the serving line with a heaping plate of food. He walked over to where Horace and Mary Jo Tremont were sitting at a table.

"Pull up a chair," smiled Tremont. "This is the best food I've eaten in a long time. The cook cost a fortune, but he's supposed to be the best barbecue artist available. What have you been doing the last two days? I expected to see you or Pawnee Joe to pay you off. Nobody could find either of you."

"I've been hiding out," Slocum said.

"Trouble?" asked Mary Jo. She was dressed in a black ankle-length skirt and a white blouse.

"Depends on how you look at things," Slocum said. "Things were getting mighty uncomfortable at the hotel."

Horace Tremont frowned. "My hotel? Ain't the help doing their jobs?"

"No complaints. But I'm not used to being hustled by people wanting me to invest in something."

Horace laughed. "You've arrived, Slocum. When drummers start coming around to sell you something, you find peace of mind is a precious thing."

Mary Jo asked, "What are they offering?"

"You name it and they want Pawnee Joe or me to invest our money."

Horace nodded. "Well, you fellows stop off at my office any time. I'll put the money in a bank account. Just tell the banker that you're John Slocum. The Bannerman boys told me you were splitting the reward twixt you and Pawnee Joe. So you can split an account of ten thousand dollars. Is that to your liking?"

"Perfect," Slocum said.

Mary Jo looked at Slocum. "I've invited a young

woman to sit with us. You don't mind meeting a beautiful woman, do you?"

"Sounds just fine to me."

Horace asked, "Who do you have in mind?"

"Carlee Loving," Mary Jo replied.

"Darn good choice," Horace told Slocum. "Nice-looking woman. Not as pretty as Mary Jo, of course, but no one is. You'll like Carlee. And while we're on the subject of money, she has plenty of it."

Slocum looked interested. "Money doesn't interest me, but a good-looking gal is a treasure I'd be willing to explore."

"Her uncle was Oliver Loving," said Horace. "Maybe you've heard of him."

"I don't recall the name."

"He was a cattle buyer."

"I should know the name," said Slocum.

Mary Jo asked, "You've been around the cattle business?"

"I rode with Charlie Goodnight on a couple of cattle drives."

"You'll get along with Carlee," Mary Jo said. "She has been thinking of getting into the cattle business. Besides, I want to leave you in good hands. Horace and I are leaving tomorrow to go to Chicago."

Slocum was surprised and said so.

"Mary Jo's idea," said Horace. "After this kidnapping we talked it over. She hasn't seen her family since we were married in Chicago. Time to get back there and renew her family ties and my friendship with them. We're taking a stagecoach to Cheyenne, then boarding the Union Pacific train to Omaha and on to Chicago."

Slocum asked, "The railroad is that far west?"

"They're laying track seven days a week," Horace said.

"We're looking forward to it," said Mary Jo. "I've never been on a train and neither has Horace."

"Mules are more my style," said Tremont.

Slocum looked up as a shadow passed across the table. A black-haired woman of medium height stood by the table. She had pale skin, high cheekbones, and lustrous black eyes. Her eyelids were dark and heavy, giving her a slack, sleepy look that was sensuous and attractive. Her lips were full and fleshy, giving her mouth a voluptuous appearance.

"Am I interrupting anything?" the young woman asked.

Mary Jo leaped up from her chair.

"Carlee! Where have you been?" Mary Jo turned to John Slocum and introduced Carlee Loving.

John Slocum stood up. "My pleasure, ma'am."

"Sit down, sit down," said Carlee Loving. Her gaze moved up and down Slocum's body. "So you're the gallant man who rescued Mary Jo. Strange, you don't look like a gunfighter."

"He's a man of many secrets," said Mary Jo. Her eyes twinkled as she looked directly into Slocum's eyes.

Carlee Loving sat down across from Slocum. She looked at the man from Calhoun County with a frank, inviting gaze. "Do you dance, Mr. Slocum?"

"John to such a pretty lady," Slocum said.

"Watch it, Carlee," laughed Horace Tremont. "This fellow acts like he's a fast shuffler."

Carlee licked her lips and gave Slocum a wanton look.

"We could use some new men in town." She laughed, a low, husky sound that came from deep down in her throat. "Denver has been awfully dull this year. I never have anything exciting happen to me. All I do is mope around the house and feel lonely. Mary Jo has all the fun. She gets kidnapped by a gang of bandits, gets rescued, and everyone in town turns out to welcome her back."

Mary Jo looked serious. "Believe me, you don't want to be kidnapped. They were planning on selling me as a slave down in Mexico."

"A love slave, I hope," Carlee smiled. "Think of lying around a ranch with nothing to do except make love a few times a day."

"You need to get married, Carlee," said Horace. "A nice man like John could make you happy."

Carlee Loving smiled at Slocum. "Do you think our friends are trying to be a matchmaker?"

"It certainly sounds like they have plans."

Carlee asked, "What about you, Slocum?"

Mary Jo giggled. "What are your plans, John?"

Slocum reddened. "Remember," he said, "I can keep secrets."

Someone slapped Slocum's shoulder. He turned and saw Pawnee Joe Miller holding a plate of food.

"Sit down!" Horace Tremont cried. "Is that your first plate?"

"Third one," said the little mountain man. "I love oysters."

Before the meal was finished, a group of musicians set up on a wooden dance floor that had been laid for the occasion. Soon the thin, sad sound of Mexican music filled the darkening evening. The dance floor became a whirling mass of spinning bodies, stomping boots, and bare-shouldered women.

Slocum danced several times with Carlee Loving, admiring her figure. Hot and mysterious, her dark eyes met his gaze with a mocking frankness. When her full lips parted, she revealed a set of perfect white teeth.

Returning to their table after the musicians took a break, Carlee asked, "Are you staying in Denver?"

"Until something interesting comes along."

"Are you going to take me home tonight?"

"I was thinking of asking."

"I'm waiting."

"May I take you home tonight, Miss Loving?"

She shrugged her shoulders. "I will think about it, Mr. Slocum."

"I will await your reply with great eagerness."

She turned her head and the light from the torches shone on her glistening black hair. An aloof expression came over her face.

"Don't get too eager, sir!"

Slocum laughed. "You should be an actress."

"Hell, Slocum, every woman is an actress. We've been acting since the first time we crawled out of the crib." Although she smiled, the tone of her voice indicated that Carlee Loving had spoken what, to her, was a basic truth.

It was late and they were dancing again. The music was a slow, soft tune that reminded Slocum of his home in Georgia. Before the War, when the South was like a timeless universe, he had attended dances and balls held in the great plantation manor houses.

The women were young, pretty, and experts at flirting. The men were handsome and carefully groomed. Everything in the plantation homes was proper and correct. The food was tasty, properly cooked. The liquor was smooth and aged. Everything was beautiful—until you peered past the façade of culture and looked at the black quarters, the human auction blocks, and the institution of slavery.

Now Slocum let go of his memories and concentrated on holding Carlee Loving in his arms.

She rested her head on Slocum's muscular shoulder. "You make a good headrest, John."

"I try to please, my lady."

"Are you experienced in pleasing women?" She looked up into his face with a wanton smile.

"No complaints from the parties involved."

"Let's say good night to the Tremonts and go to my house," she suggested. "These fools will dance until dawn. I think we can find something better to do."

They left the dance floor, thanked the Tremonts for their hospitality.

"You're not leaving until you dance with me," said Mary Jo. "Where are your manners?"

"I've been overwhelmed by Carlee's company," Slocum grinned.

"I'll stay here and have a drink with Horace," said Carlee, dropping down into a chair.

Slocum whirled Mary Jo out onto the dance floor. The music was sweet, low, like the wind moving through a high mountain pass.

"You like Carlee?" asked Mary Jo.

"She's a beauty."

"I thought it would be a good idea to introduce you two."

"Thank you kindly."

"Dear, dear John." Her hand tightened on his wrist. "At least you will have company while Horace and I are in Chicago. She's rich and pretty, John. That is a better bargain than being rich and old, believe me."

"Don't press things," Slocum said. "I've just met the woman."

"It gives you something to consider," she smiled. "If a person has to grow old, and all of us do, we might as well do it with a little wealth and companionship."

Carlee Loving's house was set high in the rolling hills above Denver, a structure of wood, native stone, and thick-paned windows. Down below, the lamps of Denver twinkled in the velvet darkness.

On clear warm nights, with the wind blowing gently down from the snow-capped Rocky Mountains, the air was thin and clear. Now, in Carlee Loving's bedroom, the atmosphere was scented with the lilac perfume worn by the young woman.

John Slocum's gaze was fixed on Carlee Loving's firm round bottom as she stood before a large mahogany dresser and mirror. The lines and curves of her body provided him with intense visual pleasure. The wanton young woman glided about her bedroom with provocative movements. She knew that Slocum was impressed with the erotic motions of her body.

Carlee splashed more perfume on her breasts. She stood for a moment, eyes closed, the golden candlelight glowing on her smooth, creamy skin. Slocum admired the rising mounds of her soft skin, the shadowed clefts, the dark glistening eyes that promised many pleasures.

Carlee Loving was certainly not an innocent woman. Not by any measure, Slocum reminded himself. She had provided an hour of diverting sexual entertainment. In bed, she was a daring person willing to try anything. She was imaginative and versatile with both her mind and body.

She was a different type of woman. What had been familiar movements, ordinary gyrations, became strangely erotic and exciting.

She was certainly not a common woman, yet she had instinctively learned the skills of a courtesan. Women like Carlee Loving, Slocum decided, caused kings to leave the queen's chamber, started wars, and were the reason behind many revolutions.

Silently, she moved over to the four-poster bed. She made a tiny, sensual sound back in her throat. The huskiness of the purring sound reminded Slocum of a female panther in heat. She lay down on the red satin coverlet, her white skin in vivid contrast to the colored fabric.

Still purring, she rolled toward Slocum. She kissed him on the neck, rubbing her thick, dark bush against his hip. The scent of her perfume seemed to heighten her female sexuality. Slocum felt lust move into his loins like a hungry beast needing a feast of flesh.

Her hand came out, fingers touching the tip of his penis.

"Such a pretty thing," she husked. "All nice and hard."

He grew and hardened under her touch. It was apparent that Carlee Loving was familiar with touching the places that made a man feel good. There was an almost professional technique in the way she stimulated him to a size, a hardness that made Slocum feel proud.

She was really a true masterpiece in bed, a delightful woman as innocent-looking as a Sunday school teacher. Sometimes the pretty ones were stuck on themselves, he thought. But Carlee Loving was intent upon providing him with a surfeit of satisfaction.

She was lovely, willing, full of life, and knew how to use every part of her body. Now, her heavy breasts were moving against his chest, the nipples lightly touching his skin. He bent his head and took the stiff pinkness in his mouth. He sucked hard. Her flesh shuddered and thrust toward him. The purring noise grew louder deep down in her throat.

"Oh, your tongue is like fire," she said.

"Umm."

"I could stay here with you forever." She pressed her body hard against him, slipping his hardness between her legs. She was hot and wet as she moved back and forth over his stiffness. She was a tight, muscular woman with strength that was surprising for someone with a small, delicate frame.

"Now, lover..." The purring started again deep in her throat, a liquid gurgling sound that was almost animal in nature. It was as if she had reverted from civilization and gone back to ancient, primeval instincts that were beyond taming.

She pressed Slocum back against the satin sheet. Her legs swung over his body and, stroking gently, she guided his ramrod erectness into her damp, moist body. Then, with a moan of pleasure, she dropped down upon him, enclosing him with her tight warmth.

Carlee Loving pressed down with her rotating bottom. He sucked her breasts with a feverish desire. She kept him inside her body, moving up and down over his hardness.

"I love you," she husked. "You're all man, Slocum."

"Quit talking."

"I want to do this forever."

"I'm about ready," he gasped.

"Any time, sweet... any time."

Then, with their bodies melded together as a single hungering flesh, they rose like climbers on a craggy mountain slope. Higher, still higher, they went until the pinnacle was attained. Together, they stood on that high peak. The sun shone, the heavens opened, and all was fair and kind in the world.

Then, holding each other's hands, they leaped off the mountain top as a climactic wave of satisfaction swept through their bodies.

Twice more that night they made love. Finally, exhausted by their physical exertion, they lay entwined in each other's arms and slept.

And Slocum, for once, did not dream.

8

Mattie Pitzen considered her existence in Denver to be something of a dream. The whole town was a wonderment, the largest town Mattie had ever seen. It was unreal, Mattie decided, how men crowded into the Paradise Saloon each night, standing elbow to elbow, drinking like whiskey was free.

Mattie was agog on the matter of money. Every man in Denver seemed to have money to eat, drink, be merry, and bed down a whore whenever the urge arose.

Back in the little cowtowns where Mattie had worked, a woman was a highly prized and salable commodity. The only trouble, besides how cowboys smelled, was their lack of hard currency. Barter was an accepted method of payment for a whore's services in those little towns. Saddles, bridles, bedrolls, rope, steers, and whatever wasn't nailed down was traded for her favors. It was either take a traded item, the saloonkeepers explained, or go hungry.

A girl could wear herself to a nubbin and never come up with a copper penny. Uneducated, Mattie could never keep track of the saloonkeeper's mathematics in selling—or re-trading—bartered items.

That was one reason why Mattie went for Frank Wylie's line about owning a ranch. They would steal a lot of money, then settle down on their own spread. At forty-one, Mattie was tired of grinding her life away without monetary reward. Whores were supposed to have hearts of gold, but Mattie didn't have a pot to call her own.

Denver was different. That was plain to see. Mattie felt guilty about going back to whoring, not taking time to mourn Frank Wylie's death. But the luckless outlaw was not much of a loss, she realized after a couple of days in Denver.

Her life had been a succession of mistakes, errors, false starts, and misplaced love. Nothing ever seemed to work out. She had never known real love nor had an enduring relationship. Maybe, just maybe, one of the jaspers who came into the saloon might take a shine to her. Then Mattie could get out of the business before old age or the pox ruined her career.

Mattie liked to get up early each morning. She was frying eggs and ham in a kitchen for the women upstairs above the saloon. She was full of hope and fairly happy for the first time in many years. She had prospects for the future, providing the U.S. marshal didn't file charges. And everyone had told her that was unlikely.

Mattie turned the sizzling food in the skillet. She heard a soft noise and turned to see red-headed Rosalie McDonald standing in the kitchen doorway.

Rosalie's eyes were bloodshot. Tears rolled down her cheeks.

"What's wrong?" asked Mattie.

Rosalie gurgled out a sob. "I got to quit working here."

"You got fired?"

"Looks that way."

"What for?"

"I caught the pox."

"Oh, Lord!" Mattie went over and put her arms around the younger whore. Mattie knew about the pox, and considered herself lucky never to have come into contact with the dreaded disease.

Some folks said it could be cured with patent medicine. Others claimed it just ate through a woman until her vital organs fell out on the floor.

Rosalie McDonald bawled some more, than sat down at the kitchen table.

"I'll fix you some breakfast, darling," said Mattie. "One egg or two?"

"I'm watching my weight. Better make it one." Rosalie sobbed again. "The hell with it. I'm not going to be working. I might as well enjoy myself. Scramble up a couple."

Mattie went back to the stove.

"That's the reason I can't work no more," Rosalie said.

"What're you going to do?"

"I don't know."

A notion formed in Mattie Pitzen's mind. "I'm making good money. I could give you enough to live on. Maybe we could get a little house or some place of our own."

"You'd do that?"

Mattie smiled. "Sure, I never had a place of my own. I'd like that. But I got in mind a favor I'd want you to do."

Rosalie's eyes narrowed. "I knew there'd be a catch."

"Nothing bad. See, I feel guilty about the way my man was killed."

"You mean that outlaw?"

"He wasn't much," admitted Mattie, "but he treated me pretty good sometimes. Anyhow, I'd like to do something for Frank—wherever he is at. Probably roasting down in hell. Anyways, I was thinking maybe you could have sex with the jasper who killed Frank."

"John Slocum?" Rosalie's face clouded. "I hate his guts!"

"That's what I mean, darling. It would make us both happy to see John Slocum with a case of clap."

Both women smiled.

Across Denver, John Slocum and Carlee Loving were also having breakfast. They were seated at a glass-topped table decorated with a vase of flowers and a white linen table-cloth. Breakfast had been prepared by Carlee's cook, served by a uniformed maid who spoke with a French accent.

"This house must cost a lot to keep up," said Slocum.

"The bills come with the territory," smiled Carlee.

"The Tremonts said you had a relative in the cattle business."

"Oliver Loving."

"I should know him."

"Oliver was a big cattle broker," Carlee explained. "He worked out of Texas and Louisiana, made a lot of money selling beef to the railroad. You've heard of the Union Pacific?"

Slocum smiled. "Once or twice I've heard mention of it."

He wondered if Carlee Loving thought he was an ignorant cowboy. Everyone knew about the Union Pacific Railroad pushing west.

"The Union Pacific is laying track around Cheyenne right now," Carlee said. "Oliver always figured he would get the contract to supply the beef herds. That's why he moved to Denver. He wanted to be right on the scene, so to speak, and Denver was situated between Texas and Wyoming."

"What happened to Oliver?"

"He was killed by Comanches. He started for Texas to line up herds for delivery this year. He was jumped by the Indians last fall."

"You were his heiress?"

Carlee Loving nodded. "I was his only relative."

Slocum glanced around the dining area. "Oliver must have done better than most people in the cattle business."

"You been around cattle?"

Slocum nodded. "Among other things. I made a couple of drives with Charlie Goodnight. We took a herd from Texas up into Kansas."

Carlee Loving's eyes brightened. She asked, "Slocum, would you like to make a lot of money?"

"Everyone has been asking me that question the last couple of days," he replied. "One gent wanted me to invest in his silver mine. Another fellow thinks big money can be made raising horses. Someone else wants me to invest in a general store. And three men want me to back them on a prospecting trip to find a diamond field. They claim to know exactly where the place is located."

"That sounds pretty good."

Slocum chuckled. "They even had diamonds that were picked up right off the ground."

"That's great."

"Except Mother Nature doesn't provide cut and polished stones."

Carlee laughed. "They showed cut diamonds?"

"Swore they were picked up right off the ground," Slocum replied. "Now, what kind of deal do *you* have in mind?"

"Cattle."

"Go on."

"As I said, the Union Pacific is up in Cheyenne. They're buying herds of beef to feed their workers. We can make big money supplying cattle to the railroad."

"Where do we get the cattle?"

"Charlie Goodnight has a herd down in Apishapa Canyon. He is waiting for a buyer."

"I don't have that kind of money," said Slocum.

"I do."

"What would this involve?" Slocum asked.

"The Union Pacific is taking bids today and tomorrow."

"Here in Denver?"

"Yes. And I think we can come in with the lowest bid."

"What makes you so sure?"

"Charlie Goodnight owes me a favor. Slocum, I can buy that herd for the right price. My concern is finding a man to get those cattle from Apishapa Canyon to Cheyenne."

"There are plenty of men who will boss a cattle drive."

"But not many I know and trust."

"You have the money to buy the herd?" Slocum asked.

"No problem."

"What about a crew?"

"I have the money to hire them."

"Would you want me to invest?" Slocum wondered.

"I'll finance the entire operation. I'll pay you to hire the men for the drive out of Apishapa to Cheyenne."

"Why do you want to do this?"

Carlee Loving's hand made a sweeping motion. "All of this takes money to run," she said. "Lots of money. Besides, I'm a young woman and I want to do something useful with my life. I don't want to just sit here and look up the hill at the Tremont mansion. I want to make money, Slocum, get involved in interesting projects. I want to make my mark in Denver. Oh, I know what people say about women staying home, not getting into business. But times are changing. It is 1867, after all, and there is plenty of money to be made out here."

"Maybe you should invest in real estate. Buy some property."

"In Denver?" Carlee pursed her lips and shook her head. "The railroad is going through Wyoming. Denver is going to die. The town with a railroad will attract the newcomers. People are scared in Denver. You haven't been here long enough to hear the rumors. The businessmen are afraid Denver is going to die."

"The mines will keep things going," Slocum said.

"What if the ore runs out?"

"Horace Tremont doesn't seem to be afraid of that."

"Horace is an old man. He has enough money to keep him in high style for the rest of his life. And money left over for Mary Jo to live in splendor for the next hundred years. Horace has made his pile."

Slocum asked, "Can I think it over?"

"Bids have to be in tomorrow morning at ten o'clock."

"I don't like making sudden decisions."

"What can go wrong?" she asked.

"From Apishapa to Cheyenne isn't the easiest trail for a cattle drive."

"You can handle any problems."

"Are you putting all of your money into this deal?" he asked her.

Carlee made a snorting sound. "Don't be silly! This won't take more than forty-five thousand dollars. I can get the herd for that. It isn't my last cent, nowhere near it. Let me worry about the money. You handle the bids tomorrow and get ready for a trip to Apishapa Canyon."

"I'll have to find some good hands."

"There are plenty of wranglers out at the stockyards."

"All right," Slocum said. "I'll do it. What kind of bid do you want me to make?"

"We can come in low with sixty-five thousand."

"Where are the bids accepted?"

"The Exchange Building."

"Verbal or written?"

"Write it down on a piece of paper."

"All right."

"You've made me very happy, Slocum." Carlee Loving rose from her chair and laid her napkin on the table. "Now, I would like to make love before you leave."

Slocum chuckled and pushed back his chair. She turned and headed for the bedroom. Slocum followed.

They lay naked on Carlee's large four-poster bed following their session of lovemaking. That particular expression was on her face: the look of a woman who has been sexually fulfilled.

Slocum started to get up. She pulled him back on the bed.

"I want to tell you things I've never told anyone," she said.

"Dark secrets?"

"My past."

He encouraged her to talk. "Where were you born?"

"Galena, Illinois. My father was a miner."

"You grew up there?"

"Like a weed. My mother died giving birth to me."

"I'm sorry."

"It was tough growing up without a mother," Carlee said. "I always felt left out. When the other kids had a party, I would be invited, but I felt alone. I didn't have a mother to teach me about life. Hell, Slocum, I can't even cook a decent breakfast."

"You're lucky to have money." Slocum thought of how his mother and father had taught each of their children to be self-sufficient. He had been taught to cook by his mother and the black woman who ran their kitchen.

"When my dad was killed in a mine accident, Oliver Loving and his wife came to Galena. They took me back to their home in Omaha. Oliver's wife was the mother I never had. She taught me how to dress, how to talk with people. She helped me get over my shyness."

"She sounds like a nice person."

"She was a jewel. Then she died, while I was attending a girls' school in Massachusetts. I didn't get back to Omaha until the end of the school year."

Slocum thought of his parents, of his brother who had died in the War. "Life seems to be handling losses," he said. "I know the only permanent thing I've found in life is change. Time goes along and people, places, and problems always change. Nothing remains the same for long."

She asked, "How do you handle the losses in your life?"

"I try to stay focused."

"What's that mean?"

"I'm like a little circle," he explained. "If your circle and my circle happen to overlap, then that is really great.

But if your circle goes away—for whatever reason—I still stay focused in my circle. It may not be the best way of living, but it seems to work for me."

"Money is my answer," Carlee said. "I want to have as much money—maybe more—than any other person in the world. What about you, Slocum? Do you like money?"

He made a shrugging movement with his bare shoulders. "I've had money and I've been hungry broke. Rich is better, but I don't get upset if the money isn't in piles and bunches." He patted her heavy breast. "Speaking of money, I have to go see Horace Tremont and collect the reward for finding Mary Jo."

"One more time," she whispered. "Let's make love again. I want to feel you inside me. I want to be united, my body and yours blended into one flesh."

Slocum smiled. "I can spare the time."

Slocum arrived back at his hotel shortly after the noon hour. He discovered that Pawnee Joe Miller was still asleep. The mountain man said he had walked a widow to her home after the party.

"It must be something about the thin air," said Pawnee Joe, splashing water onto his face from a china basin. "That's probably it, Slocum. The women get all heated up because of the thin air. Honest, I couldn't get away till the cock crowed. How did you do with that sweet-looking thing you took home?"

"Fair to middling."

Pawnee Joe wiped his face with a hand towel. "That ain't no real answer, Slocum. You're hiding something. Tell me about how she was the sweetest woman in the universe, how she was panting for you, and how you were the only man who ever satisfied her. That's what I'm asking about. I don't need this 'fair to middling' stuff. That don't make for good talking. I want to know all the details about how you loved her."

Slocum laughed. "You mean lust, not love."

Pawnee knuckled his red-veined eyes. "Whatever. I like hearing the details."

"Not now," Slocum told him. "We'd better get over to Tremont's office and pick up our money."

"You think he'd run out on us?"

"No, but Tremont is going back East for a trip."

Pawnee Joe started pulling on his boots. "So we had better collect the money before the jasper takes off."

"My exact thought."

"I'll be with you in a jiffy." Pawnee Joe shuffled over to the dresser, ran his hands over his hair.

"What're you primping for?" Slocum demanded in a tone of mock anger.

"Hell, give me a chance," said Pawnee Joe. "Never know when I'll meet up with that widow woman."

Horace Tremont was sitting at his desk when Slocum and Pawnee Joe were led into the office. The male secretary saw that they were seated, then supplied each man with a glass of prime Kentucky bourbon. When that was done, the secretary went out and closed the door behind him.

"Nice fellow," said Pawnee Joe.

"Kinda prissy," Tremont replied. He raised his glass and said, "Enjoy having you gents drop in for a drink. As for your money. . ."

"Here it comes, Slocum," Pawnee Joe whispered from the corner of his mouth.

Tremont laughed. "Go down to the bank. I've already put ten thousand dollars in the account of John Slocum.

You boys can divide it up however you see fit. Introduce yourself, Slocum, to the chief teller. He'll keep the money on deposit for you, give it to you in bills or in silver. Since I hit it rich with silver, I don't have much luck with gold. How do you like that whiskey?"

"Mellow," said Slocum.

"A long ways up the ladder from Taos Lightning," added Pawnee Joe.

Tremont nodded in agreement. "But Taos is a better brew than most men know. Uncle Dick Wooten was a friend of mine. Many a night I stayed at the San Fernando de Taos down there with his bunch. I helped him brew up a few batches. Uncle Dick knows how to make good whiskey. He could use corn or wheat, whichever was available. The trouble was that everyone wanted whiskey. There was too big a demand for the stuff. Uncle Dick could get the same money for prime aged stuff as he'd get for rotgut. After a while, he just quit caring. He quit aging to perfection and went for as strong a whiskey as he could make."

Slocum raised his glass toward Horace Tremont. He asked, "What's the worst whiskey you ever drank?"

"Had to be Tiger Spit," answered Tremont. "It would knock a man right off his feet. Two sips and you'd gag for a week."

"Blue Ruin used to do that," said Pawnee Joe. "What about you, Slocum? You must have drunk some evil poison in your wandering."

"Some stuff called the Widow Maker," Slocum replied.

After that, they started naming various whiskies they had drunk during their travels over the frontier. One was named Red Disturbance, as a result of the drinker becoming mentally deranged following a drinking bout.

There was Red Dog, Skull Bender, Apache Tears, Old Snake-tail, and Tangle Leg.

"Tangle Leg was a real pestering mess of a drink," said Pawnee Joe. "I drank some in Nevada. A local product. It had something that caused your legs to get tangled up twixt each other. But it wasn't as bad as some stuff called Knockout Punch. That was made out in California. A man got drunk one night and dropped a bottle in a horse-watering trough. When everyone woke up the next morning, the mules had drunk the whiskey. They were laid out stiff as boards."

"There used to be one down in Texas," said Slocum, "that was called Rattler's Dream. You knew you had the true goods because the maker always nailed a rattlesnake's head to the inside of each barrel. He said the rattler's head helped age and mellow the stuff."

As they talked other names came up: Miner's Lament, Mule Killer, Scorpion Soup, Good-bye Darling, Grizzly Punch, Coffin Paint, Harness Varnish, Old Copperhead, Freak Maker, and an Oregon home brew called The Baby Killer.

"Why the name Baby Killer?" asked Slocum.

"The stuff went down smooth," laughed Pawnee Joe. "But after drinking it, you couldn't raise an erection for a month."

Tremont pulled a bottle out of his desk drawer. "Listen, I know where the worst in the world was sold," he said, ever so slightly slurring his words. "I went down to New Orleans a long time ago. I got drunk down there, as was my usual habit when going into a strange town. I followed the crew of the steamboat to a cave. It was the wildest guzzle shop ever to sit on this earth. Now, these steamboaters had been dry for a while. They had a captain who believed in temperance. They wanted to get drunk as fast as possible. You know, one of those falling down, staggering to who laid the rail, kick the dog, beat up the wife and children type of drunks. Fortunately, their pets and kinfolk were back home."

"You mean they wanted to get blinded," said Slocum.

"They would have drunk mule slobber for the kick," Tremont agreed. His tongue was being loosened by the whiskey. "That saloon down in New Orleans was bigger'n any cave I'd ever been in. A real low-class dive. It smelled so bad that even the rats stayed out. Steamboaters liked the place because the main feature was about twenty addled whores. Crazy as bedbugs! I mean, you walked into that dark, dim joint and you wondered whether to stand, stomp, jump, or run. The lowest-class, nastiest-looking, most addled, meanest crowd of people I'd ever seen."

"I get your drift," said Slocum. "How bad was it?"

Tremont grinned. "It was so bad, boys, that the New Orleans temperance people held guided tours. They wanted to show where a man would end up if he kept drinking."

"That bad?" chuckled Pawnee Joe.

"Anyways, they had barrels of whiskey sitting on one side of the cave," Tremont went on. "A man laid down a nickel, picked up a tin cup, and selected his favorite barrel. The bartender kept saying you had to drink fast or the cup would dissolve."

"That is tough brew," Slocum smiled.

"Now, gents, I have drunk rotgut all over the West," said Tremont. "I've sipped in cow country, imbibed in buffalo country, and woke up naked one morning stretched out in the desert with a Methodist preacher standing over me reading the final words from his sacred text. I've never drunk anything worse than that barrelhouse stuff down in New Orleans."

"Barrelhouse Whiskey," said Slocum.

"You know the brand?" Tremont looked bleary-eyed. He poured more whiskey into his glass.

"I've heard about it."

"Those barrelhouse places were god-awful," said Tremont with a glazed look in his eyes.

Tremont rose unsteadily to his feet. He weaved to and fro for a moment, a dazed look on his face.

"Are you all right?" asked Slocum.

"I drink too much," husked Tremont. He steadied himself by holding onto the edge of his desk. "Hell to grow old, boys. Here." He took a deep breath and walked around the desk. "Let me show you boys out. I gotta go home and sleep this one off. Mary Jo and me are leaving for Chicago tomorrow."

Tremont weaved a path to the door. Slocum was tensed, ready to grab the silver baron at any sign of a fall. But Tremont staggered into the outer office without stumbling.

"Oh, Mr. Tremont," said the male secretary. "I'll have to get someone to drive you home again."

"Too damned old," said Tremont. "Too much whiskey. Too little time to enjoy my money and my wife."

"Thank you for the money," said Slocum.

"You got my wife back," Tremont said, waving his arm in a gesture of dismissal. "I owe you the thanks."

Tremont's eyes closed and he slumped down in his chair.

"He's passed out again," said the secretary.

"He do this very often?" asked Pawnee Joe.

"It has gotten worse lately. He's dying, you know, really dying. His dependence upon whiskey has reached a bad state. His whole day is spent drinking. I hope this trip to Chicago proves to be a success. Mrs. Tremont is taking him to a doctor there who specializes in people who drink too much."

"We better go." Pawnee Joe nudged Slocum's arm.

"See you later," Slocum told the secretary.

Slocum and Pawnee Joe left the office.

"That's the trouble with whiskey," said the little mountain man. "It's fun and exciting for a time. Then the stuff turns and grabs your throat."

9

Rosalie McDonald was a whore with the pox. Yet, despite her fears, Rosalie was doing all right. The bartenders at the Paradise Saloon had started a collection to help her. Rosalie was amazed to see that the customers had given two hundred dollars to the pot. That was almost six months' pay. The bartenders said they would keep the collection going for a week. The fund might grow to six, seven hundred, maybe even a thousand dollars.

Rosalie was happy because she wouldn't have to work for the money. She would not have to pretend that a jasper with a two-inch pecker was built like a bull, nor would she have to pretend that every man was better in bed than all the rest.

And Rosalie McDonald had found a true friend in Mattie Pitzen. It was awful the way Mattie had taken up with that gang of outlaws. Running with that bunch showed that Mattie was pretty loony. Or maybe there was a lack of opportunities back where Mattie lived.

Mattie was also a little backwoods in her attitude toward Denver. She thought the Paradise Saloon was the fanciest saloon in the whole world. She acted as if whoring in Denver was like being with the angels in heaven. Mattie was always gushing over how pretty everything was in Denver.

Mattie also liked the miners, prospectors, and cowboys who hung out in the Paradise Saloon. She did not see they were mostly crude men, unwashed whiskey sots with bad teeth. Mattie thought every last one was a "nice man" or "real handsome."

That morning during breakfast, Mattie was enthused about everything. "It is pure pleasure working here," she said.

"Not too bad a place," Rosalie agreed.

"I never been in a big town like this."

"It ain't that big," Rosalie said. She wondered if Mattie would start crying from happiness.

"Well, it is nice working where you don't have to compete with sheep," Mattie said.

"With what?"

"I mean, a girl doesn't have to worry about the sheep here in Denver. I ain't seen one since I got in town."

"They like sheep down your way?"

"Nobody's got any money in Texas."

"Sounds like it."

"But poor men still get horny."

Rosalie raised an eyebrow. "They never heard of Rosie Palms?"

"Who's that?" Mattie had a quizzical look on her face.

Rosalie realized the woman did not recognize the term for male masturbation. "She's just an old enemy of whoredom," Rosalie said.

"She never worked Texas."

"I'll bet she's down there working overtime. You just never met her."

After breakfast, Rosalie made another trip to the Tremont Hotel. The desk clerk gave her the same answer: John Slocum was registered as a guest. No, he was not in his room. Rosalie turned and went out to the sidewalk. She walked back to her room over the Paradise Saloon. She would keep trying to catch Slocum. That was the least she could do for Mattie: Give Slocum a dose of the clap.

The Denver Commercial Bank was identified by a painted sign in the front, hinged and swinging in the wind. Slocum held the door open while Pawnee Joe walked inside. Then Slocum followed the little mountain man into the bank. They asked a tall, thin man for the chief teller and were led to a desk and several chairs roped off from the main cages of the bank.

The man rose and extended his hand when they identified themselves.

"I'm Roger Barnett," the chief teller said. He was dressed in a black wool suit, a white shirt with a high stiff collar, a black cravat pegged with a small silver pin.

They shook hands and Barnett asked them to sit in the plush leather chairs across the desk from him.

"No problems about your money," Barnett told Slocum. "Horace transferred the sum. We have ten thousand dollars in your account right now."

"Put half of that into an account for Pawnee Joe Miller," Slocum said. "We were partners on the job."

Barnett took a quill pen, dipped the nib into an inkwell, and wrote on a white sheet of paper. Then, without speaking, he went over and handed the paper to a man working behind a regular teller's cage.

Barnett came back and said, "Congratulations, Mr. Miller. You now have an account for five thousand dollars in our bank."

"Can I get some money now?" asked the mountain man.

"Whatever sum you wish."

Pawnee Joe turned to Slocum. "How much you figure I need?"

"I'm drawing out a hundred."

Pawnee Joe looked at Barnett. "The same for me."

"I'm glad to know you're leaving most of your account in the bank," said Roger Barnett. "I know, banks fail sometimes and the depositors are left holding the bag, but carrying too much money isn't wise. Denver has a sizeable number of citizens who'll kill for a lot less than five thousand. And, of course, the Denver Commercial Bank is backed by the Tremont silver millions. You've made a good choice."

Barnett returned to the working side of the bank. He returned with a handful of gold coins and silver dollars for each man. Then, slowly and with great care, he counted out the stacks of coins.

"Much obliged," said Pawnee Joe.

Slocum asked, "Can you direct me to the Exchange Building?"

"Up the street a block. You can't miss it. The name of the building is carved in granite over the front." Barnett looked directly into Slocum's eyes. "That's where the Exchange and Businessman's Bank is located. I hope you're not changing banks."

"I'm planning to bid some cattle deliveries this afternoon. I've been told the Union Pacific is looking for cattle to be delivered in Cheyenne."

"Dear me," said Barnett. "This sounds like trouble."

"Bidding cattle?" Slocum was surprised.

"Manley Breedlow handles those contracts."

Slocum asked, "Who is Manley Breedlow?"

"A local cattle broker. He usually gets the low bid on a U.P. contract."

Slocum nodded. "Maybe Breedlow needs a little competition."

"He wouldn't think so."

Slocum pointed out that the United States and territories were a free country.

Barnett nodded his head in agreement. "But Manley Breedlow wouldn't see your bid that way. Breedlow usually tries to muscle out his competition. Fact is"—and here Barnett's voice dropped to a whisper—"Breedlow's competitors have a habit of running into bad luck. Real bad luck."

"The permanent kind?" Pawnee Joe asked.

"Ambushes, Indian attacks, things like that," whispered Roger Barnett. "Nothing can ever be proven, of course, but folks talk about it. Sheriff Ben Fillmore can't charge Breedlow with murder if a bunch of Indians kill his competitor. Yet, things have happened in the past that give people something to wonder about."

Slocum looked troubled. He wondered if Carlee Loving was as innocent as she appeared. Was Carlee using him as her pawn in a complex struggle for power and money? Did she know what happened to Breedlow's competitors? Or was the young banker across the desk simply a gossiping rumor-monger?

"I just wanted to warn you," said Barnett, as if reading Slocum's thoughts. "A man needs to know what he's getting into."

"Drop it, Slocum," urged Pawnee Joe. "We got plenty of money."

"No, I'll go over and make the bid," said Slocum. "We'll see what comes after that. Maybe I'll be the man to change Breedlow's luck."

"Or he may change yours," said Roger Barnett.

The chief teller stood up and extended his hand. "Whatever you decide, you have a friend at this bank. And, of course, with Mr. and Mrs. Tremont. I'm pleased to meet both of you."

The Union Pacific meeting was being held on the second floor of the Exchange Building. John Slocum had parted company with Pawnee Joe Miller, who was looking for a new pair of boots and some "store-bought clothes."

Slocum walked up the stairs of the Exchange Building. A long hallway ran both ways along the second floor. A hand-lettered sign directed him to a medium-sized office that had a desk at the front of the room. The rest of the office was filled with chairs.

Slocum took a seat and glanced around. He wondered if the bidding was being held some other place. He was about to check when a middle-aged man walked timidly into the office.

"Well, I was in error. I thought Manley Breedlow would be the only bidder," said the bespectacled man. He wore a gray suit. His glasses rode low on his nose. He walked up to Slocum and said, "I'm Austin Tully, an attorney with the law firm of Barlow and Thomas. Our offices are in Omaha. One of our clients is the Union Pacific railroad."

"John Slocum." The man from Georgia extended his hand.

"Are you a cattle broker?" asked Tully.

"Yes, I'm thinking of making a bid."

Tully nodded his head in agreement. "Good! Good! The railroad likes to have competition on the bidding. That is the precise reason I was sent out here—to get more cattlemen to bid on our contracts. In the past few months, Manley Breedlow has been the only broker making a bid. I'm glad to see you, young man, and I encourage you to tender a bid. Do you have cattle available?"

"A fair-sized herd."

Austin Tully rubbed his hands together. "Good, good! Most of the bidding has been on an unofficial basis. Dave Needles, our chief cattle buyer, puts out word that we're in the market. Breedlow is about the only man who does any bidding. I felt an official bid situation was called for. I rented this office and furniture. Sealed bids will be accepted until four o'clock this afternoon. Is your bid written out?"

"No, sir."

"There is pen and paper on the desk," said Austin Tully, taking Slocum's arm and guiding him to the desk in the back of the room. "We need Charlie Goodnight's herd delivered to Cheyenne. Write down your delivery price at the railhead."

Slocum sat at the desk and wrote out his proposed bid:

The Goodnight herd delivered to Cheyenne for
$65.00 per head.
Total cost: $65,000. John Slocum.

Austin Tully stood in the center of the room so he could not see what Slocum had written.

"Use one of those envelopes," said the lawyer. He motioned to a stack of U.P. envelopes on the corner of the desk. "Seal it and give it to me."

Slocum followed the attorney's instructions.

Austin Tully accepted the envelope and tucked it into his inside coat pocket.

"Thank you," he said. "Now, what do you think about linking our nation with a railroad? Isn't that a magnificent undertaking?"

The two men were still talking about the marvels of a transcontinental rail linkage when footsteps sounded in the hall outside the meeting room.

Two men came sauntering through the door. One was a short, compact man with red hair. He wore a gray business suit similar to the suit that Austin Tully had on.

"Well, I wondered if you gentlemen were going to make it," said the lawyer, pulling a gold watch from his pocket. "Five minutes until we open the bids."

Tully made the introductions. The small man was Dave Needles, chief cattle buyer for the Union Pacific railroad. He was a homely-looking man with ears that were too large for his head. His eyes were anxious, always darting about, never looking Slocum straight in the face. Slocum noticed another trait that revealed Needles's nervousness. The cattle buyer always ran his thumb up and down the fingers of his right hand.

"Mr. Needles ordinarily handles our bid openings," said the lawyer. "He is headquartered at the railroad."

Austin Tully beamed as the two men shook hands.

"And this gentleman," said Tully, "is Manley Breedlow. He is Denver's only cattle broker. Leastways, he was until this afternoon. This is John Slocum, Mr. Breedlow. He is going to bid on our contract."

Manley Breedlow was a tall, muscular man. His features were scarred by a red slash that started on the bottom of his chin and ran down the side of his neck. His brown hair was carefully clipped, worn short and oiled. He wore a pair of stockman's trousers, a twill shirt, and a black string tie held together with a gold medallion. A Colt six gun rested in a hard leather holster tied on his right hip.

Breedlow did not offer to shake hands.

"You're bidding on this contract?" Breedlow's dark eyes stared menacingly into Slocum's face.

"I've considered it," Slocum answered. He could feel the resentment and see the anger in Breedlow's face.

"You have to be careful with this kind of bid," said Breedlow, ignoring Slocum and talking to Austin Tully and Dave Needles.

"Mr. Slocum seems all right," said Tully.

"He can screw up a good bid letting," Breedlow went on. He turned to Slocum, anger flaring in his eyes. "Where are you getting your cattle, Slocum? What guarantees does the Union Pacific have that you will actually deliver the herd?"

Slocum bristled. "Watch your talk, Breedlow."

"Yes," said Austin Tully. "The questions you've raised, Mr. Breedlow, are concerns of the Union Pacific railroad. They are not questions that should interest you."

Manley Breedlow's jaw jutted out in a defiant gesture. The scar on his chin reddened. He stared at Austin Tully for an instant, appeared ready to strike the attorney. Then Breedlow took a deep breath and the tension left his body.

"I was just looking out for the railroad."

Austin Tully turned to Slocum. "Do you have the funds?" the attorney asked.

"Yes."

Tully nodded. "Slocum's word is good enough for me." He pulled out his gold watch and flipped open the case. "It looks as if the time has arrived to accept bids," he said. "Are you bidding this afternoon, Mr. Breedlow?"

Manley Breedlow's eyes glittered with anger. He pulled an envelope from his hip pocket.

"I've put down a sensible price," he said.

The envelope was passed to Austin Tully, who said, "Mr. Slocum has already handed in his bid. Mr. Dave Needles and I will go to the desk and open the bids."

The cattle buyer, Dave Needles, had remained silent during Manley Breedlow's statements. The position of his stance, and the way he looked at Breedlow, indicated to Slocum that Needles was somehow in cohoots with the cattle broker.

Austin Tully and Dave Needles walked to the front of the room. The attorney removed two envelopes from his inside coat pocket and laid them on the desk. The two men sat down in chairs behind the desk.

"Time to open the bids, Mr. Needles," said Austin Tully. He looked across the desk at John Slocum and Manley Breedlow. "You gentlemen might as well sit down."

Slocum eyed Breedlow with undisguised contempt. "Take a seat."

"Don't tell me what to do," snapped Breedlow.

"Gentlemen, sit down so we can open the bids," said Austin Tully. "I will not stand for any foolishness. This is a simple business transaction. All of us concerned know we're bidding on the herd that Charlie Goodnight is holding down in Apishapa Canyon."

Slocum and Breedlow sat down.

"Open the first bid, Mr. Needles," said Austin Tully.

Dave Needles tore open the envelope. He withdrew the sheet. "This is a bid from Manley Breedlow. He will deliver the herd to Cheyenne for one hundred thousand dollars."

"The other bid," said Austin Tully.

Dave Needles opened the envelope. "John Slocum's bid is for sixty five thousand dollars."

"What the hell—" Manley Breedlow's body stiffened.

"Go on," said Austin Tully.

"The low bid has been handed in by John Slocum," intoned the cattle buyer. "The contract is awarded to Mr. Slocum."

"Well done," said Austin Tully with a smile of approval. "Let's fill in the written contract right now, so Mr. Slocum can hire his crew and get started to Apishapa Canyon."

The lawyer's words fell heavily on Manley Breedlow's ears. It wasn't possible for a man like Slocum to come out of nowhere and underbid him on the contract. Breedlow started to get up, easing his hand toward the butt of his holstered pistol. He could claim that Slocum had started to draw on him.

Suddenly there was a rustling sound. Manley Breedlow looked over and stared into the barrel of Slocum's sixgun. Slocum had somehow drawn the gun, but kept his draw hidden from the view of Austin Tully and Dave Needles.

"Keep your hands nice and high," Slocum said in a low whisper. "We don't want trouble, do we?"

"No." Breedlow's face was chalk-white.

"Let's don't disturb the U.P. people by getting upset."

"Oh," rasped Breedlow, "I'm not upset." He couldn't take his gaze off the gun. His eyes were fixed on the opening of the barrel.

Slocum whispered, "I thought you'd feel that way."

"Well, I had better get going," said Breedlow in a normal voice. "No use hanging around here since I've lost the contract."

Austin Tully nodded in agreement. "We encourage you to bid on the next contract," he said. "It is to the benefit of the company to have as many bidders as possible."

"Thank you," said Manley Breedlow. He turned and whispered from the side of his mouth, "Slocum, I'm going to dance on your grave. I'll see to it that you never get that herd to Cheyenne."

Then Breedlow rushed out of the office. Slocum heard his heavy boots thumping hard on the stairway as the man hit the street. A slight smile tugged the edges of Slocum's mouth. It was apparent that Manley Breedlow was used to getting his way in most matters.

Slocum walked into the lobby of the Tremont Hotel with the contract folded and tucked in his hip pocket. He was thinking about the problems connected with meeting the terms of the contract. He walked up the stairs and opened the door of his room.

A red-headed woman was lying on his bed. She was totally naked.

Slocum blinked his eyes for a moment. Then he realized the woman was Rosalie McDonald, the whore from the Paradise Saloon.

"Come on in, handsome," Rosalie said.

Slocum closed the door and came into the room. "I thought you were mad at me," he said.

"Well, what you said to me wasn't very nice."

"I apologize."

"I thought you would." She smiled and moved her body so that her large breasts rolled with an enticing motion. "I got the afternoon off. I decided we should get to know each other. No need for me giving up a handsome gent like you. Get your clothes off, honey, because this is the day that Rosalie is free. All you can handle and any way you want it."

Slocum walked to the side of the bed and stroked her

firm thigh. "You're a mighty generous woman."

A tiny smile tugged Rosalie's full, fleshy lips. "A girl has to give a man whatever she can. What I got to give you, Slocum, is something real special."

Slocum sat down in a plain-backed chair and rested his booted heels on the mattress.

"What caused you to change your mind?" he asked.

"I just got to thinking about you." Rosalie's tongue moved slowly out of her mouth. The pink tip moved sensuously over her lips.

"I'm glad you remembered me."

"Just consider this an early Christmas present. Something that Rosalie and Mattie cooked up special for you."

"How is Mattie?"

"Loving every minute of her new life in Denver." Rosalie moved from the center of the bed. There was a pronounced swelling beneath the buttons of Slocum's fly and Rosalie found herself almost looking forward to having his fleshy lance probing her innermost regions—her diseased regions.

She fought back a shudder and made a beckoning motion with her fingers. "Come on to bed, Slocum. I'm getting real hot watching you. I can see that looking at me is doing the same to you."

Slocum stood and gently shook his head. "Sorry," he said.

"Sorry?" Rosalie bolted upright in the bed. Anger and fear merged to raise a fine gooseflesh on her breasts, and her nipples jutted defiantly. "What are you saying?"

"Another time." Slocum reached out to brush her cheek, but Rosalie slapped his hand aside.

This was something she hadn't anticipated. Rosalie had never been turned down before and it seemed incomprehensible that a man, especially one sporting such an obvious erection beneath his trousers, would deign to reject her now. She fought to regain her seductive calm.

"Now Slocum," Rosalie tried in her huskiest voice, "I don't make this offer lightly. Just drop your pants and let your pecker point the way."

"It's not a compass." Slocum stood as he spoke. "Sometimes it points in the wrong direction."

Rosalie sprang from the bed, both hands clenched. "Damn you, John Slocum, fuck me or I'll kill you!"

Slocum caught her right arm, but allowed its momentum to continue unchecked, spinning Rosalie's body completely around until she was facing the bed. Then he gave her a shove, forcing her face down into the mattress, where she collapsed in tears.

Slocum picked up the chair and carried it to the other side of the bed, where Rosalie sobbed into the bedsheets. He sat down straddling the back and resting his arms on its top.

"I've seen a lot of looks from a lot of women who were inviting me into their beds for a lot of different reasons," Slocum told her. "But I never had anybody say she wanted me with such an obvious hatred burning in her eyes. Care to tell me about it?"

Rosalie told him the whole story. When she was finished, John Slocum didn't know whether to be angry or comforting. He settled for angry.

"Give Mattie my best," he told her as he walked out the door.

10

Carlee Loving greeted Slocum with a cry of pleasure. She took his hand and led the way to her bedroom. Slocum kicked off his boots and stretched out on the top of the coverlet.

"Tell me all about the bid," Carlee said. "Did we get the contract?"

Slocum turned his body. He pulled the folded contract from the back pocket of his trousers and tossed it on the bed.

Carlee snatched up the document with a cry of pleasure. Her eyes scanned the pages.

"Exactly right," she said, pleased. "Sixty-five thousand on delivery, and Charlie Goodnight will sell for forty-five thousand. That's a net profit of twenty thousand."

Slocum looked directly into Carlee's beautiful face.

"Why didn't you tell me about Manley Breedlow?" he asked.

"He's just a cattle broker."

"I hear his competition has a way of ending up dead." Slocum sat up on the edge of the bed. "You didn't give me all of the details. Why not?"

Carlee shrugged. "You might not have gone along."

"Breedlow is a bad sort. I expect trouble."

"He wouldn't dare. After all, this is 1867."

Slocum shook his head. "Breedlow's kind always mean trouble. A bully is still a bully, whether you call him a cattle broker or a businessman."

Carlee brought her face close to Slocum's. "He wouldn't dare touch either of us."

"I wish you'd told me about Breedlow before we got into this. And what about Breedlow's arrangement with the U.P. cattle buyer, Dave Needles?"

Carlee looked bewildered. "You think they're working together?"

"I'm pretty sure."

"Is there any way of proving it?"

"They've probably covered their tracks pretty good," Slocum said thoughtfully.

Carlee said, "You're not backing out? There is a penalty clause in this contract. We also have a delivery date. This is my first business venture. I don't want to lose. I want to . . ." She stopped talking and looked at the name on the contract. She went pale and her expression turned to anger. "This contract is in your name!"

Carlee Loving slammed the document down on the bed. She looked drained of life.

Slocum watched her with a wary gaze.

"The U.P. would probably not do business with a woman," he said. "Besides, you didn't say anything about whose name was supposed to be on the contract. I didn't even think about it."

Carlee Loving got up from the bed. She paced the carpet, wringing her hands.

"I don't know what to do," she told Slocum.

"I'll try to have the name changed in the morning."

"No!" Her voice was shrill. "That might cause trouble. Especially with Manley Breedlow's being angry. Christ! How did we ever get into this mess?"

"You wanted to make some money."

"True!" she said quickly. "That is the entire reason for getting involved. We want to make money. So, Slocum, we're going to be partners in this venture. We'll split everything right down the middle. How does that sound?"

"Fair as can be," he agreed. "I never thought about my pay."

"There's just one little catch," Carlee said.

An alarm bell went off in Slocum's mind. "What's that?"

"You're going to have to pay the wranglers for driving the herd to Cheyenne. How much will that cost?"

"I have enough to cover it. What about paying Charlie Goodnight for the herd?"

"I have that here," said Carlee Loving.

She went over to a tall wardrobe dresser, opened the door, and brought out a black patent leather satchel. She threw the bag in Slocum's direction. He grabbed the edge of the satchel. It fell on the bed with a heavy, thudding sound.

"Open it," Carlee commanded.

Slocum undid the lock. He drew back the leather sides and saw that the satchel was crammed with gold coins.

Slocum whistled.

"I went to the mint this afternoon," Carlee said.

"There's exactly forty-five thousand in gold in that bag. Charlie Goodnight doesn't trust paper money."

Slocum said, "Paper money isn't worth much in Texas, but everyone understands the value of gold."

Carlee Loving began to unbutton her dress. "This calls for a celebration, Slocum. How about it?"

Slocum left the Loving mansion as the clock was chiming eleven that night. Half an hour later he was in his hotel room. Five minutes after that he was fast asleep.

Slocum awakened early the next morning. He had breakfast with Pawnee Joe Miller in the hotel dining room. Over eggs, bacon, and pancakes, the two men discussed the cattle drive.

"You want in?" Slocum asked.

Pawnee Joe shook his head. "I've got plenty of money in that bank account," he said. "No need to start scratching for more until that starts petering out. Speaking of petering out, I saw that red-headed whore from the Paradise looking for you yesterday. From the looks of your face this morning, I'd say she found you."

"She did," admitted Slocum.

"Any good?"

"Fair to middling."

Pawnee Joe chuckled. "That bad, huh?"

"Let's just say that she has something that a self-respecting man would do well to stay away from." Slocum took a slug of coffee. "Sure you don't want to come along on the drive? I could sure use a couple more good hands."

"Christ, Slocum, I'm getting old. My idea of a good time is not sitting in a saddle all day with a horse between my legs."

"Want to help me hire a crew?"

"That I'll do. Hiring a crew doesn't take much traveling. We ought to find a good bunch out at the stockyards. Probably plenty of hands out there willing to work hard, sleep alone, and do it for practically nothing."

The stockyards were on the edge of Denver, a series of corrals, sheds, and barns. The Stockman's Inn was located across from the yards. The restaurant and saloon was a hangout for cattlemen, wranglers, and anyone looking for a job.

Slocum and Pawnee Joe walked into the dimness. They waited a moment inside the door, letting their eyes adjust to the darkened interior. A couple of tables were occupied by men playing cards. Two men were standing at the bar, drinking coffee and looking as if they had slept outside the previous night. Bits of straw and dead grass clung to their shirts.

The bartender came over with a bored look on his pasty white face. "Help you, gents?"

"We're looking to hire some wranglers."

The barkeep waved his hand around the room. "Take your pick."

"Who would you pick?"

"I'd start with Jimmy Long and Earl Doolittle. They're the two standing at the end of the bar, the ones with the straw on their clothes. They're stuck in Denver without jobs. Good men, just nothing in their line of work."

"I don't want bottle babies," said Slocum.

"They drink," answered the bartender, "but it ain't their occupation, if you know what I mean."

"I do."

"Want me to send them over?"

"I'll wait outside. I don't want anyone to overhear our talk."

"Gotcha!" The bartender winked and walked toward the two wranglers.

A few moments passed while Slocum and Pawnee Joe waited outside in the cool morning air. The door opened wide and the two sleepy-eyed men came out.

"You're looking for hired hands?"

"That's right," Slocum said.

"I'm Earl Doolittle," said the blond-headed man. He was tall and lean, and his trim body looked ready for a long ride. "This is my partner, Jimmy Long. We've been riding together for almost four years."

"Ever drive cattle?"

"Hell, yes. From Texas to Kansas."

"Like the work?"

"It beats starving," grinned Jimmy Long. He was a short, stout man with an animated face. He looked like the kind of man who could be depended on in a tight spot.

"Fifty bucks for helping me drive a herd from Apishapa Canyon to Cheyenne."

"Can you give us about ten dollars in advance?" asked Doolittle.

"What's the problem?" Slocum asked. He wasn't comfortable with making a payment in advance of the work.

"We got a feed bill and a bar bill," said Jimmy Long.

"Fair enough. I'll pay them."

Jimmy Long asked, "You hired a cook yet?"

"Nope."

"I'd like to recommend Carlos Rivera. He's around here someplace. Used to cook a couple times when we made a drive from Texas. A good man, neat and clean."

"Tell him he's hired. Have him make out a list of provisions for seven men."

Long asked, "How many more you need to hire?"

"You boys are the first."

"Give us a half-hour," said Earl Doolittle. "We'll round

you up the best crew you ever seen. The yards are full of good men, and they're all looking for work."

By noon, Slocum had hired a crew of wranglers. Carlos Rivera, the cook, was a fat, jolly man with a big belly, stocky legs, and thick arms. He had signed on and made up a list of provisions. He also knew where a chuck wagon and team was located. The rig and mules could be rented for a reasonable price for the cattle drive.

Fred Tumwater was a middle-aged cowboy with a thick head of salt-and-pepper hair, a hangdog appearance, and a roping ability that would stop a bull. Tumwater had protested, but finally consented to give a demonstration of his skill with a rope. Tumwater was an outstanding rope handler. He agreed to handle the strays during the drive.

Herb Norris looked to be about thirty-five years old. He wore a battered brown hat, tweed trousers, and a ragged calico shirt. His boots were old and heel-worn and their leather was cracked. He looked like a bum, but everyone vouched for his savvy with cattle.

"I grew up down in Texas," Norris said. "Never knew nothin' but the cattle business. Thing I never learned was how a man could make a livin' raisin' the blamed things. That was before the railroads come through to the West and made a market for beef. If you want somebody to look pretty on your drive, I reckon I'm not your man. But I can sure punch the back end of a steer, move a herd in the right direction. I am braggin' some, but I am a dang good point-man."

The hired hands met that morning in an empty barn at the stockyards. Slocum went over the situation for them, explaining where the herd was located, the problems with moving the cattle north.

"And we can expect some two-legged rats trying to stop

us," Slocum told the men. He wanted to be truthful with the group. "You may be called on to do some shooting. Any man wants to drop out now, I'll just ask for him to keep his lips closed. Nobody's going to mind if you figure this is my fight. Fifty dollars isn't very much money. You shouldn't have to die for it."

"These people," said Fred Tumwater. "Do we know any of them?"

"I won't mention names. I don't know for sure."

"Sounds like Bart Redfern's bunch," said Earl Doolittle.

"Who's he?" Slocum asked.

"A noted cattle rustler," Doolittle said solemnly.

Everyone laughed.

"I think you mean notorious," said Jimmy Long, grinning.

"Maybe so," Doolittle agreed. His face was red from bashfulness. "All I know is what I hear from people. There is talk that Redfern and his bunch are roaming around this area. Maybe talk of Charlie Goodnight's herd got them moseying around. They were up by Cheyenne for a while, sneaking cattle away from the corrals at night."

"What about guns and ammunition?" This came from Carlos Rivera. "I cook and don't like to even think of fighting. Too much belly!" He stroked his ample stomach. "But if we're going to have trouble, I'd feel safer knowing we got guns and ammunition."

"Write down what you want," said Slocum. "The rest of you give your needs to Carlos. He can get the guns when he picks up the grub and supplies this afternoon."

"When do we leave?" asked Herb Norris.

"As quickly as possible," Slocum answered.

"Is he going with us?" Norris pointed to Pawnee Joe Miller.

"Hell no," answered the little mountain man. "I ain't fool enough to go traipsing off to Apishapa Canyon when Denver has beds. And some of them beds have women in 'em."

"First smart man I met all day," said Norris, grinning.

Slocum cautioned the men to be tight-lipped about their plans. "If there are rustlers around, we sure don't want to get them thinking about an ambush," he explained. "The less folks know about our plans, the better off we'll be out on the trail."

After the meeting, Slocum led the men over to the Stockman's Inn and bought them all steak and eggs for lunch.

He was pleased with the progress that had been made that morning. He still wondered about what Manley Breedlow planned on doing, if anything. There was always the possibility that Breedlow was a blowhard, a man who didn't back up his words.

He also wondered if leaving the satchel of gold with Carlee Loving had been wise. Someone might have seen the young woman enter or leave the Denver mint. Hardcases would kill their mothers for a handful of gold. The Lord only knew what they would do for a leather satchel filled with forty-five thousand dollars in freshly minted gold pieces.

Immersed in his thoughts, Slocum's eyes took on a distant look. He was brought back to the present by a nudge of Pawnee Joe Miller's elbow.

"You still with us?" Pawnee Joe asked.

"Sorry. I was thinking."

"Just so it doesn't get to be a habit," said Pawnee Joe. He looked up with a bright expression. "Here comes our food, boys. Let's eat!"

* * *

Slocum spent the afternoon purchasing supplies and equipment for the cattle drive. After a quick dinner in the hotel dining room, he rode out to Carlee Loving's mansion.

Carlee was in an anxious mood. She paced the richly carpeted floor of her main parlor with a nervous step. She did not seem to be concentrating on Slocum's words, although she answered his questions in a routine voice.

Slocum gave her a goodbye kiss and rode back to town. He left his horse at the livery stable and crossed the street, headed for his hotel. He was unaware of the two men until their figures loomed up directly in his path. A warning went off in Slocum's mind.

The two men were undoubtedly brothers. Their facial features held a strong resemblance; they were both redheads, almost carrot-topped. They were about twenty years old, dressed in old jeans, tattered calico shirts, heel-worn boots.

But the guns holstered on their hips were Colt .44s, well oiled, with bone handles.

Both men were standing in the end of an alley. Their hands were dangerously close to their guns. Their eyes had a bright, shiny glint.

They had the look of amateurs. Their holsters were not tied down. The pistols were worn at an angle that would slow up a draw.

"Don't—" Slocum began.

One man went for the draw. He was a bit taller than his brother and stood closest to Slocum.

Slocum went into a tight, taut fast draw.

A change came into the eyes of the red-headed stranger. The young man knew he had lost. His eyes widened with fear, but he kept pulling out that big sixgun.

Off behind, Slocum saw that the second man had become scared. He was already turning to flee down the alley.

Slocum's pistol came free of the holster.

He waited a half-second, hoping the young man would do something—anything. His mind screamed to end the game.

But the kid's big pistol was still coming up.

Slocum fired. Orange flame blasted out of the pistol barrel. The acrid smell of gunpowder tinged the air.

The impact of the bullet drove the young man back into the alley. He was knocked back against a brick wall.

He stood there for a moment, trying to keep on his feet. The man's fingers relaxed and the Colt dropped into the dust. Both hands clawed the brick wall in a futile attempt to remain erect. Then he fell back onto the muddy ground.

He whimpered.

Slocum looked around. No one was coming. The second man had vanished from the alley.

Slocum looked down into the wounded man's face. "Son, you've got about five minutes left," he said. "Who hired you to do this? Was it Breedlow?"

"Don't know any Breedlow."

"What's your name?"

"Bill Tucker." Beads of sweat popped out on the young man's forehead.

"Who was your partner?" Slocum wanted to know.

"My brother, Vince. He said you'd be easy."

"Who said that?"

"Man who gave us thirty in gold to put your lamp out."

"A name would help, Bill. You've not got much time left. There's a hole in your back the size of my fist. You're filling up with blood."

Slocum's shot had slammed in under the ribs and came smashing out below the left shoulder blade. Slocum could hear the blood whooshing from an artery near the heart.

"Needles hired us," Tucker coughed.

Slocum was puzzled. "Needles? Dave Needles?"

"God, yes. That was him, mister. He said you'd be a pushover. Get me a doctor. Can't you help me? I don't want to die! Jesus, I'm sorry."

A bright intensity came into Bill Tucker's eyes. He coughed, then started gasping for breath that would not come. He whimpered. Then his body went limp and he was quiet.

Slocum looked around for eyewitnesses. No one was in sight. He left Bill Tucker's body and walked out of the alley. Dave Needles was the chief buyer of beef for the railroad. He should be above reproach, although a lot of men have a buying price. Maybe he was in cahoots with Manley Breedlow.

Maybe that was why the lawyer, Austin Tully, had been sent to Denver. Breedlow and Needles were gulling the company with overpriced bids. Breedlow had braced him, yet Needles had hired a couple of amateurs to put Slocum against a wall. It looked like some kind of game to get money from the railroad.

Slocum also knew that Vince Tucker, the dead man's brother, would have to be hunted down. He would be burning with hate against Slocum. Turning and running out of the alley would shove a lot of guilt into Vince's mind. Somehow he would rationalize that it was Slocum's fault.

In addition, Vince Tucker was in danger from another element. When Dave Needles learned that the job to kill Slocum was botched, the U.P. cattle buyer would want Vince Tucker killed. A man who can testify against you in court has to be silenced. Slocum figured this would occur to Dave Needles, who would try to protect himself by killing Vince Tucker.

Slocum moseyed through the saloons that evening looking for Pawnee Joe Miller. He also asked about the Tucker brothers. Men in the Larimer Street and Curtis Street saloons knew the Tuckers. They said they rode with a bunch of hardcases led by Bart Redfern, a notorious cattle rustler. Redfern and his bunch usually hung out at the Bucket of Blood Saloon.

Slocum didn't relish walking into a saloon full of hardcases and asking questions. That was a sure way to end up ventilated by lead. Instead, he went to the hotel in hopes of finding Pawnee Joe. He figured the little mountain man might be able to shed some light on the puzzling developments.

It was possible that Slocum was putting Carlee Loving in danger. It had probably not been wise to leave the bag of gold at her house. But now the whole area of the cattle drive seemed more complicated. It was possibly a conspiracy, a crowd of people involved in rooking the railroad. Yet it was difficult to figure out who was the mastermind behind the whole affair. Manley Breedlow, likely.

As Slocum entered the hotel lobby, the clerk motioned to him.

"A letter for you," he explained, handing over a plain white envelope with Slocum's name written on the front in black printing.

Slocum opened the envelope and read:

Get out of Denver, Slocum.
Don't bring a herd to Cheyenne.
A friend

The warning was printed on a sheet of the kind of plain white paper that could be purchased in any general store or print shop.

Slocum asked the desk clerk, "Did you see the person who left this letter for me?"

"Sure," answered the man. "It was one of those kids who hang around the saloons and run errands."

"Know his name?"

The clerk shrugged. "Just one of those kids."

"Could you recognize him if you saw him again?"

"I might. Is it important?"

"If you see him, let him know I have a silver dollar for him for delivering this."

"I'll be sure to tell him," said the clerk. "But this was a new boy. He may or may not come back."

The action was getting crazier, Slocum decided. He walked out of the hotel lobby and down the street. Why would a man like Dave Needles hire two gunmen to keep Slocum from bringing the herd out of Apishapa Canyon? After all, one contract should not be a life-or-death matter.

Why not back off, miss one contract, and then go back to doing business again in the same way?

And if Dave Needles and Manley Breedlow were partners in the scheme, why did Needles hire the Tucker brothers? They were rustlers rather than real gunmen. Breedlow would know some real hardcases who were capable of taking out any man.

Slocum went back into the saloons again. At least he could have a beer while thinking about the situation. He was in the fourth saloon, sipping his drink, when an old man sidled up beside him.

"I heard you're looking for the Tucker boys," the old man said, talking from the side of his mouth.

"Yep."

"What's it worth to you?"

"What're you asking?"

"I know where they've been holed up this past week.

Heard you was asking about 'em. Then, not more'n ten minutes ago, the sheriff's deputies found one of them boys all stretched out in the alley dead. I heard you asking around. That oughta be worth a ten-dollar gold piece. Seeing I know how to keep my mouth shut, not mention anything to them Bannerman brothers. They're the deputies with those sawed-off shotguns."

"I know the Bannermans," said Slocum. He reached into his jeans and pulled out a gold piece.

"Lou Shipley's the name," said the old man. "I'm a prospector."

"Glad to meet you, sir."

"Pleasure's mine," said Shipley. "Now, Vince Tucker is holed up at an old shack on Arapahoe Street. That's just beyond the stockyards. He don't want anyone to know he's there."

"How'd you find him?" asked Slocum.

"That shack belongs to me. But I married a widow woman and moved into her house." Shipley smiled. "My new wife doesn't like me lifting a few brews now and then. I hid some dust when I left the shack. That poke is my drinking money. Never had any trouble because it was hid real well. No trouble, that is, until this evening. I started to get my dust and this Tucker boy was there, scared to death. He put a pistol to my neck, told me to get packing. I didn't stay around to argue. That feller is ready to blow holes into anybody who walks up to him. Be careful if you go visit."

"I will," Slocum promised.

"I would be very careful," said a man who was standing behind Slocum.

Turning around, Slocum saw with amazement that two other men had been listening to the conversation. They were hard-looking young men with unkempt beards and long hair.

"We should have palavered some other place," said Shipley.

"Hell, don't worry about it," said the taller of the two strangers. "I knowed them Tucker boys. No-good trash. Never did a day's work 'cepting if it was thievin'. Then, they'd work like dogs to take someone else's property. 'Sides, neither of them boys are very fast with a gun."

"True," Shipley agreed. "But I wouldn't want to walk into a dark shack knowing someone inside had a gun."

Slocum was dumbfounded. He thanked the old prospector for the information and went out into the street. Amateur or not, Slocum didn't plan on surprising Vince Tucker in the dark. He went back to his hotel and slept until early morning.

11

Slocum waited until morning before checking Lou Shipley's shack. A heavy rain had fallen during the night. The air stirring around Denver carried the sweet, damp smell of wet earth and grass. The ground underfoot was soft as Slocum rode out Arapahoe Street.

Past the stockyards, the buildings thinned out. The first place was a cabin, a small barn, and a corral. Wisps of thin woodsmoke rose from the structure's rock chimney. A cow chewed grass in a pasture back of the house, her bell clacking melodiously in the warm morning air.

Out of the barn came a large collie dog. The dog crossed the front yard and sat waiting beside the wooden steps. The door opened and a small, bearded old man stepped out. He carried a tin bucket. He paused for a moment, took a deep breath of the fresh mountain air, then started out to milk the cow.

The old man stopped in mid-yard, seeing Slocum riding up.

"Howdy," said Slocum. "This is a fine morning."

"Reckon it is," the old man answered in an amiable voice.

"I'm looking for Lou Shipley's place."

The old man pointed down and across the road. "That place over there," he said. "But you ain't goin' to find Lou there."

"He said I could use the place for a while."

"Lou's always been a generous fellow," said the old man. "Did all right by himself. Married a widow woman, Mrs. Nickols. Used to be Adam Nickols' wife, 'fore he got kicked in the head by his favorite mule. Adam was always a hard worker. Left his wife pretty well off. He'd be spinnin' in his grave if he knew that a boozehound like Lou was spendin' his money."

"I take it you don't approve of Lou."

"Nothin' to me." The old man looked directly at Slocum. "I mind my own business. Live pretty good out here. Might say that things're gonna be crowded in Lou's cabin."

"Why is that?"

"Well, some other fellow is staying there. I'm the sort that tries to be a good neighbor. Bossy"—he jerked his gray head toward the pastured cow—"gives more milk than me or the dog can handle. I seen this young fellow over there. Walked over with a pail of milk to give him. That was last night. Unfriendly sort. Yelled at me and swore he'd shoot me if I came back."

"Sorry to hear that," said Slocum.

"It was almost dark last night when a fancy rig came by and turned in over there. Prettiest carriage I seen in a long time. Horse looked like a thoroughbred."

"Lou's place must be popular."

"Drawing the wrong kind, I'd say." The old man's face brightened. "You want to stick around, I'll have some sweet milk from Bossy in a few minutes."

Slocum thanked the old man, and said he'd have to stop over at Lou's place.

"Just be careful," came the advice. "That kid over there has the willies."

The sun came down strong and bright as Slocum rode toward the weathered shack belonging to Lou Shipley. The building had been erected hastily and without attention to appearance. Fir logs had been placed around a rude framework, then chinked with clay. A rock chimney sat on one side of the structure. Like many settlers' homes in the wilderness, the shack did not have any windows. However, gun holes had been bored in the dried clay on each side of the house.

Slocum dismounted and, warily, walked toward the shack. The front door was swinging to and fro in the wind. The rusty hinges made a grating sound.

Slocum drew his sixgun. He walked along the side of the house.

His booted foot came up and kicked back the door. The door slammed hard against the inside wall.

Silence.

Holding his pistol at shoulder height, ready to pull down on anyone or anything, Slocum stormed into the cabin.

Vince tucker lay on a corn shuck pallet before the fireplace. His eyes were closed, his mouth slack and open. He had the appearance of a young man sleeping off a night of carousing. Except for the hilt of a long-bladed filleting knife that protruded up from Tucker's stomach. Dried blood crusted the front of the dead man's shirt.

Slocum caught sight of a white scrap of paper pinned to the front of Tucker's shirt.

"You are next, Slocum."

The note was printed in the same block letters as the note left at his hotel. The writing was neither cursive nor distinctive. Slocum pulled the first note from his hip pocket. He compared the two pieces of paper. They appeared to be identical. The two notes must have been written by the same person.

Slocum put the two pieces of paper in his pocket.

He gazed down at Vince Tucker's features. The face was taking on that white, waxy pallor of dead men. Already the blood had drained from his body, crusted his shirt.

Slocum glanced around the interior of the cabin. The sparse amount of furniture—a chair, table, a small stool—were all upright and looked undisturbed. Apparently Vince Tucker had known his killer. No signs of a fight could be discerned by Slocum. He wondered how a petty drifter like Vince Tucker could know someone rich enough to own a fancy rig pulled by a thoroughbred horse.

Slocum studied the room for some clue to the killer's identity. Nothing seemed to be out of place.

Then Slocum noticed that the dead man's left hand was clenched tight. He went over and pried open the cold fingers. A scrap of lace lay in Vince Tucker's dead palm.

Slocum picked up the scrap and wondered if Vince Tucker had been trying to leave a message. Maybe the killer was a fancy dressed gambler who favored frilly lace-trimmed shirts. A man like that would probably own a fancy carriage and a handsome horse.

Slocum slipped the piece of lace in his front pocket.

"Good luck," he whispered to the dead man.

Slocum walked out the door and started for his horse.

He heard a noise behind him, started to draw his pistol as he spun around.

"That's far enough, mister," said a steady, calm voice. "You freeze right there. You're under arrest for murder."

Slocum felt a gun barrel press against his back.

"Who are you?" he asked.

"I'm the United States marshal."

"Tom Jackson," Slocum recalled from his conversation with Sheriff Ben Fillmore.

"You're a killer, Slocum. Why did you knife that jasper in there?"

Slocum did not reply. He felt the gun barrel push harshly against his back.

"Answer me," the marshal snapped.

"I didn't kill him."

"Were you tied in with him?" The gun barrel was shoved against Slocum's back again.

"No."

"Are you hooked up with Bart Redfern and his gang of rustlers?"

"Marshal, I think Sheriff Ben Fillmore will vouch for me. Look, Jackson, you've got the wrong man. I didn't kill Vince Tucker."

"Oh, now you know his name. I expect you were the one who gunned down his brother last night."

"Don't be ridiculous."

At that instant, something rustled in the weeds off beside where the two men stood. Slocum took a chance. He could sense that Tom Jackson, the U.S. marshal, was distracted. This intuitive notion came from a decrease in the pressure of the gun barrel against his back. The man's attention was on whatever man or animal was moving through the weeds.

Slocum spun around, bringing up his arm to deflect the marshal's. The marshal made a little grunting sound as Slocum's fist slammed against his forehead. The lawman's pistol dropped to the ground as the shock of the blow knocked him senseless.

Slocum reached down for the pistol. Out of the corner of his vision, he saw that Tom Jackson was a young, well-dressed man with a muscular build. He also noticed that the U.S. marshal was coming to his senses.

Slocum's fingers touched the butt of the marshal's pistol.

A booted foot came crashing down on Slocum's left wrist. As Slocum's right hand came across to grab his throbbing wrist, Tom Jackson scooted back across the wet, muddy ground.

Slocum spun around and kicked out at the lawman.

He missed Jackson's body, lost his balance. Slocum went down in the mud.

He saw Jackson scrambling to his knees. The marshal's eyes were fixed on the pistol lying on the ground. Slocum was in an awkward postion. He didn't have time to draw. His hand shot out and his fingers tightened on the lawman's arm.

Slocum jerked back with all of his strength.

Jackson came crashing back against Slocum's body.

The two men locked arms and wrestled in the muddy yard. Slocum was on his back, looking up at Tom Jackson. The marshal's face was contorted by anger and pain. His eyes held a glazed, intense wildness.

"You bastard!" roared Jackson.

He drew back his arm, balling his hand into a massive fist.

Slocum's hand shot out across his chest. He drove his fist into the marshal's testicles.

A wild scream ripped out of Jackson's mouth. He howled as his hands went toward his groin. Jackson's body arced up off Slocum's chest.

Slocum moved rapidly, spun around, and slammed his body against his opponent. Now Jackson wavered and then went back into the mud.

The marshal was just about to give up when his fingers felt the steel of the pistol barrel. He grabbed the gun and brought it up, aiming the butt for Slocum's face.

Slocum ducked his head and the butt smashed hard against his shoulder.

Slocum cried out in pain. Then he clenched his teeth and drove his fist toward Jackson's face.

Slocum's blow connected with the marshal's jaw. A stunned, numbing sensation spread up Slocum's arm. His fist hurt. One finger was throbbing, stabbing pain.

The marshal's head snapped back. His body started to slump as he fell back in the mud. Then Slocum straddled the lawman. Slocum's control snapped and everything in the world seemed to vanish. The whole universe was this lawman and Slocum's need to win out.

Tom Jackson saw the fanatical look in Slocum's eyes. He began to edge back away.

"Take it easy," said Jackson. He spit blood off to the side.

"I'm gonna kill you," husked Slocum. He took a deep breath and tried to stand up.

Jackson's boot shot out and crashed against Slocum's ankle. Slocum came crashing back down onto the ground. The lawman's fist slammed against Slocum's ribs. Jackson howled with glee when a whining sound of pain came from Slocum's lips.

"Hurt, you devil! Hurt!"

The lawman snapped another blow into Slocum's rib-cage.

"That'll teach you to take on a U.S. marshal!" Jackson's fist came back to deliver another blow.

Slocum roused himself, rolled over, and scrambled to his feet. He wondered what two adult men were doing fighting like crazed savages on muddy ground. He snapped a hard jab into Jackson's windpipe.

The marshal's face contorted as he gasped for air. His face turned red, then darkened. He made little strangling sounds, trying to draw air into his lungs.

While the marshal fought for breath, Slocum stood up on shaky feet. He felt weary. It seemed as if every inch of his body was racked with pain.

Slocum picked up the marshal's pistol. He looked down at the lawman, who was making convulsive sounds as he tried to gain breath.

Then Jackson's eyes reddened as he caught the first lungful of air.

For the longest time, the man lay there and drew air into his body. Although the act of breathing was painful, Tom Jackson never inhaled anything sweeter than the morning air of Denver.

Slocum made a motion with the pistol.

"Get your ass back in the cabin," Slocum said.

"I suppose you're planning on killing me," said Jackson. His voice was high, shrill. The act of speaking bothered his vocal cords. He coughed.

"I got the right," said Slocum, herding the man toward the open door of the cabin.

"Where did you learn to fight like that?"

Slocum inhaled a deep breath. "I was in the War."

"A reb, no doubt." Tom Jackson crawled into the doorway of the cabin. He stopped. "Jesus! I can't go any further."

"Move it or I'll kick your ass the rest of the way," said Slocum.

"Let me get . . . my breath!"

"Move, Jackson."

The man crawled a few inches farther into the cabin. Each movement of his arms was accompanied by a wheezing sound from his lungs. Once, his body went through a convulsive movement and the lawman fought back the urge to vomit.

Tired, but content with his victory, Slocum reached down and grabbed a handful of the lawman's coat. Staggering under the weight, but unwilling to show his weakness, Slocum steeled himself and lifted the dead weight of Jackson's body into the cabin.

They rested in the gloomy interior, both men seeking to regain their dissipated strength. Jackson lay face down on the rude plank floor, his head cradled in his arms. Slocum slumped back in the chair, resting his arm on the worn table. His hand held the lawman's pistol.

The only sound in the room was that of heavy breathing.

At length, a collie dog came cautiously through the doorway. The animal sniffed the air, then walked over to where Tom Jackson lay on the floor, pressing his nose against Jackson's face. He made a low, sorrowful whining sound.

Tom Jackson made a chuckling sound.

"I know how he feels," the lawman said. "Jesus, Slocum, every bone in my body is aching."

"Me too," sighed Slocum.

Jackson tasted the bile in his mouth. He raised his head and spat into the fireplace. "You fight pretty good."

"The same to you."

"I never had a man catch me off guard."

The collie left Jackson and went over and sniffed at

Slocum's mud-splattered leg.

Slocum said, "Nice dog. Tell your friend there is a first time for everything."

"The dog was in the weeds," Jackson said.

"I know."

"That's what caught me off guard."

"Blame it on the dog," Slocum chuckled.

"Damned right. I ain't facing up to you being the better man."

"Lord, I'm not. I got pain on top of my pain."

Jackson raised his head. He stared straight ahead at the lifeless body of Vince Tucker.

"Who killed him?" Jackson asked.

"I don't know. I know I didn't do it." Slocum was getting back his normal wind. "How did you end up out here?"

"I got a note that you were going to kill Tucker."

"Who said that?"

"It wasn't signed."

"Who delivered it?"

"It was shoved under my door. The person knocked and then ran off before I came out."

"So you hot-footed it over here and waited until I came out."

"That's about it."

"I wonder what I'm going to do with you," said Slocum with a long sigh.

"I don't like the thought of ending up like the lately deceased lying here. I prefer any other alternative."

"I got to keep you on ice for a spell."

"How about my promise to keep my distance?"

""I don't let my life rest on any man's word."

"C'mon, I was an officer in the War."

"Yankee?"

"Of course."

"Then I'll have to tie you up."

"Just be out of town when I get free," Jackson warned him.

"I told you I didn't kill him." Slocum glanced at Vince Tucker's lifeless corpse.

"Not that," said Jackson. "I'll kill any man who makes me the laughingstock of Denver."

"I need twenty-four hours."

"To kill some more? Christ!" Tom Jackson moaned as he rose to a sitting position. "Slocum, you're bad news. You're to be commended for getting back Mary Jo Tremont. That Wylie gang was a bad bunch. Not because they were tough and wild. They were just low-class, brutal men. We don't need that kind in the territory. I heard about the run-in you had with Manley Breedlow. And then Bill Tucker ends up dead in an alley. The next thing is you're asking around about where his brother Vince can be found."

"Someone is setting me up," said Slocum. "That's the way I figure it."

"Who?" Tom Jackson's head was pounding.

"Probably Manley Breedlow."

"I wouldn't put it past Breedlow," Jackson agreed. "Are you going down to Apishapa Canyon and get that herd from Charlie Goodnight?"

"I plan to, yeah."

"When are you leaving Denver?"

"I got things to do before I go."

"Like what?" the lawman asked.

"Have a showdown with Breedlow." Slocum rubbed his hand over his bruised lower lip.

"How long will that take?"

"I'll be on the trail by tomorrow morning."

Tom Jackson nodded. "I promise to stay out of your way until noon tomorrow."

"And what if you don't?"

"I'll give you some information that might benefit you." Jackson spat into the fireplace.

"Hell, I don't want to kill you. I'm taking your promise. What's the information?"

"Jubal Thorne and Harold Ackerman are in Denver."

"The hardcases?" Slocum whistled. "The last I knew they were in Dodge City."

"Something's brewing."

"You think so?" Slocum straightened up in the chair.

"They've been hanging around Denver for about a month," said Jackson. "I understand they found work as bodyguards for Manley Breedlow. They went to work for him yesterday."

"Denver is a magnet for hardcases."

"Yep. Bart Redfern's bunch is in town. Add Jubal Thorne, Harold Ackerman, and—oh, yes, we can't forget you, Slocum. It looks like Denver is going to have a show-down." Jackson looked over at the corpse of Vince Tucker. "What I'm trying to figure out is who is on what side. Plus what the whole thing is about."

"I'm trusting you," said Slocum. He stood up, feeling the pain all over his body.

He handed the sixgun back to Tom Jackson.

"A deal is a deal," said Jackson. Still sitting on the floor, he shoved the pistol into his holster.

12

Slocum and Tom Jackson drew a bucket of water from the well at Lou Shipley's shack. They washed the mud and blood off their faces, then tried to remove the grime and dirt from their clothes. Slocum finally gave up and decided his clothes needed a good laundering.

Tom Jackson polished his U.S. marshal's badge, cleaned and oiled his pistol. He kept trying to pick little pieces of mud from his clothing. Slocum noted that Jackson was fussy about his appearance, something Sheriff Ben Fillmore had mentioned.

The sun was near the noon mark when Slocum rode down to the stockyards. He stopped and checked with Carlos Rivera, his cook for the cattle drive. Rivera reported that all the supplies, equipment, guns and ammunition were stowed and ready.

Jimmy Long and Earl Doolittle strolled up while Slocum was talking to Rivera.

"When are we leaving?"

"Tomorrow morning," Slocum answered.

"We're itching to go," said Jimmy Long.

"Yeah, but word is out that we're going," added Doolittle. "None of us mentioned it to anyone. So it had to come from someone else."

"The rumors say when we're leaving?" asked Slocum.

"Nope," said Long. "They just know we're going."

The other wrangler drifted over to the chuck wagon. Slocum spent the afternoon checking equipment and paying off bar and feed bills for his crew.

Carlos Rivera demanded that Slocum and the rest stay for supper. The Mexican was proud of the chuck wagon. "Cowboys used to carry a little food in their saddlebags," said Rivera. "They ate cold food for three or four days. It was Charlie Goodnight, the man we're getting the cattle from, who invented the first chuck wagon. Mr. Goodnight wanted his men to have hot food every day."

Rivera was proud of the chuck wagon. As the others gathered around the wagon, he showed the spices, flour, coffee, sowbelly, and other foodstuffs stowed in the bins and compartments. A large pot box hung under the rear axle. It carried the dutch oven, skillets, and other utensils.

The wagon would be a general utility vehicle for the cattle drive. Rivera had purchased shovels, axes, tents, bedrolls, and tarpaulins for the drive.

Slocum discussed the coming drive with the wranglers while Rivera cooked up their dinner. They sat down to a meal consisting of fresh beef, boiled cabbage and potatoes, plenty of cornbread, and sourdough biscuits.

"And for dessert we have Spotted Pup Pie," announced Rivera, spooning out a pie containing rice and raisins.

Slocum finished his meal and washed his tin plate, cup, and utensils in the dishpan behind the chuck wagon. Then he told the crew to be ready to pull out the next morning.

Swinging back aboard his horse, Slocum rode back into Denver. He headed for the Brown Palace Hotel, where Manley Breedlow had a room. The Brown Palace was the most spacious, luxurious hotel in Denver. Slocum felt uncomfortable walking into the lobby. His clothes still contained bits and pieces of mud from his fight with Tom Jackson. The other people in the lobby were elegantly dressed.

Slocum spotted Manley Breedlow standing in the lobby. Breedlow was puffing on a long cigar, talking in an animated manner to two men. Slocum recognized the men with Breedlow as Jubal Thorne and Harold Ackerman.

The two gunmen were well dressed and well armed. They wore black coats, starched white shirts with the lacy frills fancied by gamblers. This garb was adorned by dark burgundy-colored bowties with gold ornaments. Their faces were lined by weathered ruts, their large mustaches looked untrimmed and bushy. While Breedlow's hair was impeccable, Ackerman and Thorne both had long sideburns that had an unkempt look. Their boots were in need of a shine.

Despite their appearance, Slocum knew Jubal Thorne and Harold Ackerman to be cool professional gamblers and gunmen. They had the instincts of rattlesnakes and were quick to take offense for word or deed.

Jubal Thorne was in his forties, a man known throughout the West for his ability with a sixgun. He turned his head as Slocum walked through the lobby, a sneer on his lips.

"Gentlemen, look what the dogs have brought in," said Thorne, motioning toward Slocum with his cigar.

"Well, hello, Slocum," said Harold Ackerman. "I heard you were in Denver. Still stirring up trouble? You always were a pissant for messing in everyone else's business."

Manley Breedlow turned to face Slocum.

"My new associates," said Breedlow. "I believe you have been previously acquainted with these gentlemen."

"Hello, Harold," said Slocum. "Are you still slipping hole cards up your sleeves?"

"Go to hell, Slocum," snarled the gunman.

"And here's ol' Jubal," Slocum said with a thick drawl. "The last time I saw you, Jube, you were swamping out saloons for a glass of rotgut. I take it someone helped you to get over that affliction."

"One more word . . ." Harold Ackerman's face turned dark with anger.

"Let's don't get to fighting," said Manley Breedlow with a mirthless smile. "Have you changed your mind about the cattle contract, Slocum? I am willing to give you a small cut for turning the contract over to me."

"No deal," said Slocum. "I just came to ask you about a couple of men who stopped breathing recently, Vince and Bill Tucker."

Manley Breedlow's face turned chalk white. For an instant Slocum thought Breedlow would lose control. He was on the verge of starting to say something, his mouth open, mind racing.

Just then, a uniformed bellman walked up. He leaned over and whispered into Manley Breedlow's ear.

"Thank you," Breedlow said.

Breedlow ignored Slocum and turned around just as a young woman of obvious breeding came across the lobby.

"My apologies," Breedlow said to Slocum. "I have to cut our conversation short. I have a previous appointment." Breedlow's gaze moved up and down Slocum's frame.

"You are going to have to get another tailor, Slocum. You're starting to look like the dogs have been playing with you in the mud for a week."

The young woman opened her arms in a welcoming gesture as she glided across the lobby toward Manley Breedlow. She had strong, firm features that were enhanced by the creamy texture of her skin. A lady, Slocum thought. Her complexion was delicate, as was the pale greenness of her eyes, and the smile on her glistening lips was intriguing, beautiful, and serene. She moved with the gracious motions of a gentlewoman, someone who was obviously accustomed to wealth and beauty.

Her hair was the color of honey, hanging back over her white shoulders in carefully arranged locks. Slocum noted that the expensive gown she wore was not gaudy, but expertly tailored to conform to her hourglass figure.

She was standing beside Manley Breedlow and her thin hand was held out.

Smiling with smug satisfaction, Manley Breedlow took the young woman's hand. With an exaggerated gesture, Breedlow leaned over to kiss her hand.

As Breedlow bent over, the young woman looked at Slocum with her warm, sensuous eyes. Her look was inviting, a hint of warm pleasure that could be found by her side. There was also a glint of amusement in those pale green eyes. They seemed to say, *isn't Manley Breedlow an obvious but charming fool?*

Slocum took a step forward. He tapped Manley Breedlow on the shoulder.

"Breedlow, you didn't answer my question," said Slocum. "Do you know anything about the killing of the Tucker brothers?"

Manley Breedlow shot up like a spring-loaded knife blade. His eyebrows dropped into a scowling position, his eyes clouding with inner rage.

"Sir! Your business with me is concluded," snapped Breedlow. He turned slightly toward the young woman. "I suggest that you take up the question with Thorne and Ackerman."

Then, shutting his mouth grimly, Manley Breedlow took the young woman's arm. They started to glide through the lobby toward the dining room.

Slocum stared after them, his mouth open, his gaze fixed on the movement of the woman's hips. Then he started forward to resume his questioning of Manley Breedlow.

Suddenly his path was blocked by the looming bodies of Jubal Thorne and Harold Ackerman. Both men stood above Slocum's height and they were heavier, more muscular.

Slocum forced a little grin.

"Well, did you boys know the Tucker brothers?"

Jubal Thorne looked grim-faced.

"First, we ain't boys, Slocum," said Thorne in a menacing voice. "And, second, we don't know any Tuckers. Now you start for that door or you're going to have daylight streaming through your shirt."

Slocum managed a weak grin. He noticed that people in the lobby were staring. He stepped back and saw that both Thorne and Ackerman's hands were moving closer to their pistols. Their movements were slow, almost undetected.

"I guess a man could use some fresh air," Slocum said. "I think it may be time for me to relax."

The two hardcases stared at him without expression.

"No sense of humor, huh?"

Walking jauntily and whistling a cheerful tune, Slocum crossed the lobby and went out the door. He was not about to go up against Jubal Thorne and Harold Ackerman together. They were brutal gunfighters with a reputation for trickery. He figured the two hardcases had been ordered out of Dodge City, had drifted into Denver and found employment with Manley Breedlow.

Slocum was also intrigued by the two gunmen's fancy shirts, the lacy ruffles. He wondered if Vince Tucker had tried to save his life by grabbing out as either Thorne or Ackerman moved in. He was also preoccupied with the thought that the Tucker brothers might somehow be connected with Breedlow and Needles through the two gunmen.

After leaving the Brown Palace lobby, Slocum went across the street and slipped into the front of an alley. It was growing dark now. The sun was falling behind the mountains with a final burst of twilight purple.

He waited for almost an hour. Darkness came over the city and the air became cooler. His vigil was successful when he saw Jubal Thorne and Harold Ackerman come lumbering out of the Brown Palace lobby.

Slocum watched as the two men mounted their long-legged Morgan horses. They were intent on talking between themselves. They did not look back as they rode away from the hotel.

Slocum slipped out of the alley and climbed aboard his horse. Staying back, he followed the two men to Larimer Street. They rode to the end of Larimer and reined up in front of a large two-story house with red lights in the windows. Slocum watched as Jubal Thorne and Harold Ackerman tied their horses to the hitch post. Then the two men strolled into Merry's Pleasure Emporium, a well known bawdy house.

Slocum hid his horse in a grove of trees located across the road from the whorehouse. He crept into position and watched the front entrance. He was able to see quite well as a result of the lanterns lighting up the front entrance of the house.

The next person to arrive was Dave Needles, the cattle buyer for the Union Pacific railroad. Slocum drew back into the foliage as Needles paused on the front porch of the bawdy house. The cattle buyer looked around nervously, then seemed content and entered the building.

Moments later, a muscular man with a sixgun worn low and tied down came riding up. Slocum remained in hiding, uncertain whether the man might be meeting Needles and the hardcases. The man wore a leather vest and looked surprised when a groom came up and took the reins of his horse.

Something was brewing, Slocum figured. Whatever it was, it probably had something to do with the U.P. cattle contract. Manley Breedlow should be at any meeting of the group, but he had apparently been too enchanted by the mysterious young lady.

After the stranger entered the bawdy house, Slocum left his hiding place and circled the building. He discovered a back stairway attached to the rear. The steps led up to a landing that ran along the back entrance on the second floor.

Carefully, Slocum tiptoed up the stairs and crept along the landing. He heard the sound of men's voices coming from behind a shaded window. The discussion was about money.

Slocum heard Dave Needles's voice.

"I want this Slocum taken care of," Needles said. "I don't care how you do it, but it has to be done. Otherwise the whole scheme is going to fall apart. Don't you agree with me, Redfern?"

Slocum realized that the stranger who had entered after Needles was Bart Redfern, the cattle rustler. He was the leader of the gang that had included the late unlamented Tucker brothers.

"It doesn't matter to me," Redfern replied. "One way or another, I'm going to get that herd."

"Yeah, Needles." It was the voice of Jubal Thorne. "You want Slocum put away, you have to pay."

Needles spoke up. "You get five hundred each."

"A thousand and a cut of the herd," said Harold Ackerman.

Needles countered, "A thousand and no cut. You take care of Slocum and Bart and the boys will be there to take over the herd. Right, Bart?"

"Suits me," Redfern replied.

"When does Breedlow take over?" Ackerman asked.

"Hell, he has a buyer lined up right now," said Needles. "Bancroft is going to pay one hundred thousand dollars when he sees Breedlow and his wranglers driving that herd up the Platte River."

Slocum, hunched down beside the window, decided that Bancroft must be a wealthy cattle buyer. He heard a movement in the yard below.

A man shouted up. "Hey, you! What are you doing up there? Get down here this instant!"

Slocum spun around and looked down into the yard. The groom who had taken Bart Redfern's horse was staring up at him.

Suddenly the talk in the shaded room ended. Boots sounded on the plank flooring inside the bawdy house.

Slocum stood up and moved across the landing as a door opened in the second-floor hallway.

"Stop him!" The cry came from inside.

Slocum started down the back stairs, taking four steps at a time.

He heard the back door open, the whisper of metal sliding out of a leather holster.

Slocum hit the ground running. A bullet zipped through the air as a pistol blasted behind him. Another shot exploded. Slocum heard the thud of a bullet smashing into a nearby tree.

A third shot sounded. Dust splattered beside Slocum, who zigzagged out of the red lantern light and into the darkness. He raced to the grove of trees where his horse was tied. He leaped into the saddle and the animal lunged to life, racing toward town.

Behind him Slocum saw the orange blossoms of pistol shots. He heard men shouting, recognized the noise of men mounting their horses. Then he let the horse have its lead. He was swallowed up by the darkness in another minute.

Slocum knew he was marked for killing. It would be foolhardy to go back to his room at the Tremont Hotel. The hardcases from Dodge City might be laying in ambush. Dave Needles, Breedlow, the hardcases: everyone was stirred up and wanted a piece of his skin.

It was foolhardy to hang around Denver.

Slocum rode out to Carlee Loving's mansion. He reined in and walked up on the porch and knocked. The door was answered by the woman who acted as housekeeper for Carlee.

"Miss Carlee isn't home," the woman said.

Slocum looked puzzled.

"But she told me to give you this bag." The woman grunted as she handed the bag of gold to Slocum. "And you're to get this here note."

Slocum thanked the woman. "Could I come in and read the note? The light isn't too good out here."

"I reckon."

Slocum stepped inside the house. The foyer was illuminated by a large candelabrum.

He tore open the envelope.

See you in Cheyenne, Slocum. I'll be waiting for you! Hurry!—Carlee.

Slocum said good night to the housekeeper. He took the bag containing the gold, got back on his horse, and rode toward the stockyards. With luck, he could get the wranglers on the trail before daybreak. It was a long ride to Apishapa Canyon, and coming back with the herd wouldn't be an easy job.

13

Ten days after leaving Denver, Slocum led his wranglers
into the mushrooming new town of Trinidad, Colorado.
The trip had been uneventful, except for their first night
out. Then, a gang of night riders had come into their camp.

Slocum had exercised caution, however, in selecting the
campsite. They had stopped on a rising knoll protected on
three sides by boulders. Slocum also posted several warning lines, ropes and tin cans, around the entrance to the
campsite. The first raider's horse went down when the
ropes trapped the animal's legs. The tin cans made a loud
noise, awakening Slocum and his men. The night riders
had quickly withdrawn when Slocum's group started firing
into the darkness.

Slocum figured the raid was led by Jubal Thorne and
Harold Ackerman, acting on orders from Manley Breedlow. After the raid, Slocum led his group as if they were

soldiers in enemy territory. They holed up during the day and traveled by night.

The trip had frazzled the nerves of Slocum's wranglers. They were edgy from the night travel. Carlos Rivera, the cook, was upset because Slocum had not allowed him to prepare a hot meal. As a result, Rivera was sullen and the wranglers were angry.

Reaching Trinidad, they camped in the shadow of Fisher's Peak and rested. Slocum knew that the men needed a night in town. Carlos Rivera prepared their first hot meal. They ate and, while the cook remained in camp, Slocum and the others rode into Trinidad.

The town was booming because new settlers were moving into the Purgatoire River valley. New businesses were starting up. Saloons, gambling dens, and music halls were filled with men searching for recreation and excitement.

Slocum and the wranglers had several rounds of whiskey in the Raton Saloon and Dance Hall, the largest establishment in town. Slocum's group crowded into the bar, took a table, and watched several dancing girls on stage flaunt their legs and breasts in a seemingly unrehearsed version of hurdy-gurdy dancing.

The women were attractive, the music was loud, and the patrons of the Raton Saloon were pleased with the performance.

"Listen, Slocum," Jimmy Long said, casting an appreciative gaze at a leggy redhead who returned his look invitingly. "Me and the guys were thinking . . . it's gonna be a long ride, and this might be the last chance we'll get to . . ."

Slocum cut him off with a laugh. "Enjoy yourselves," he said, "but save a little energy for the morning."

As the men dispersed, Slocum settled back into his chair and raised his whiskey glass to his lips. He was completely unprepared for the firm package that planted herself in his lap, causing him to spill his drink down his chin and onto his shirt.

"What the—"

"Hi, sweetheart. Miss me?"

Slocum looked into the dancer's green eyes, then lower, at the ample cleavage that threatened to split the front of her colorful dancing dress. He'd never seen the woman before in his life.

"Every minute," he answered.

The woman leaned forward, hugging Slocum's neck and placing her lips close to his left ear. "I need your help," she whispered.

"What kind of . . ."

"Oh John," the girl shrieked, then tittered in amusement. "You're so bad." Then she leaned in again. "Please follow me up to my room. I'll tell you there."

"No problem," Slocum agreed.

Her dress made a seductive swish as she slid her round bottom out of Slocum's lap. She grabbed his hand and playfully led him to the foot of a staircase along one wall of the saloon and said loudly, "Come on, John. It'll be just like old times."

Halfway up the steps she paused and asked in a low tone, "By the way . . . what *is* your name?"

"John'll do fine," Slocum answered with a grin.

Once Slocum and the dancer were secure behind the closed door of her room, she became flighty and nervous. With shaking hands, she opened a bureau drawer and removed a bottle of whiskey, which she uncorked and turned up to her lips. After a satisfactory draw, she held out the bottle to Slocum.

"Maybe later," he said. "Care to fill me in on what I've just become a part of?"

"I'm sorry," the girl said. "My name's Sally Reed, but everybody here calls me Dolly. Dolly LaRue. Sort of a stage name, you know?" She took another pull on the bottle. "I heard you and that crew with you are driving some cattle up north. That true?"

"Might be. Is it important?"

"I need somebody to take a message to Denver for me. I can make it worth your while."

"Look, Dolly . . ."

"Sally."

"Whatever. We're not the Pony Express. I don't even have any idea how long we'll be in Denver, and I'm sure to be too busy to look up an old boy friend—"

"Girl friend, actually," Sally said. "She used to work here with me, and I think she may be in a mess of trouble. I just need you to warn her."

"Warn her? About what?"

Sally set the bottle on her bureau and carefully removed her shoes. The red blisters revealed by the action showed Sally Reed was a working girl who spent a lot of time on her feet instead of on her back. "It's really too complicated to get into now," she started. "Let's just say that Lottie— Lottie Catron's her name, or one of her names, anyway— got hooked up with some fellow one night and ended up taking off with him. Cooper, the man that owns the Raton, got real mad. Said he'd kill 'em both if he found 'em."

Slocum laughed. "Look, that's probably just a lot of talk. If everybody who made the same threat carried it out there wouldn't be anybody left to do the burying."

"Just the same," Sally went on, "I'd feel a lot better if I could warn her. I mean, she was kind of hard to get along with, but Lottie was about the only friend I had."

She turned away with the last bit of information, embarrassed to be revealing so much to a stranger. Slocum felt sorry for her. Young, pretty—hell, beautiful by anybody's standards—Sally was more than likely a simple farm girl who had been seduced by tales of the wild frontier. Once on its doorstep, she found herself alone.

"Why couldn't you tell me this downstairs?" Slocum asked.

"I didn't want Cooper to hear. I had to make him think we were . . . you know."

"Intimate."

Sally smiled. "Actually, I thought I was pretty convincing."

"Convinced me," Slocum told her. "I guess it couldn't hurt to drop off a message, if you want to write it out and tell me where I can find your friend."

"That could be a problem," Sally confessed. "I'm not real sure where she's at. But I'm pretty sure it's in Denver."

"You expect me to go to every door in the city?"

"Look," Sally said, suddenly calm, "if you take the message, then I know I've done all I can do. I can live with that. And I know Denver's a big place, but you might just run into her somehow. I believe a lot in fate and destiny. You almost have to around here."

Slocum found it impossible to refuse, though that had been his intention. But as he opened his mouth to tell Sally Reed to find another man, he caught sight of a glistening sparkle in her sensuous eyes and a slight tremor in her full lips. He found himself agreeing to be her messenger to Denver.

"I guess you'd better write out the note and tell me how to recognize this Lottie," he said.

"Later," Sally Reed told him, unbuttoning the few fasteners that held her dress together. "They'd be suspicious if you showed up downstairs too quickly. And anyway—"

She peeled away her outer layer to reveal delicate under-garments. "I did promise I would make it worth your while."

What the hell, Slocum thought, feeling the familiar tug-ging in his loins. It was going to be a long ride, and this might be the last chance he'd get.

Sally Reed may have started as an innocent farm girl, but Slocum was to learn how extensive her education had been. She let loose a passionate moan, and Slocum could tell that she was nearly as aroused as he.

"Ready, John?" she asked. Without waiting for an an-swer, Sally brought her hips up to Slocum's fleshy dagger and impaled herself with a swift plunge. Once situated, she paused, letting Slocum appreciate fully the wet velvet tun-nel he had entered. Then slowly, rhythmically, she began to grind her pelvis into his, an act that brought beads of per-spiration to her forehead and her breasts. Slocum watched as her bosoms bobbed, undulating with the motion of her fluid hips.

Occasionally a cry would form in Sally's throat, only to be choked off before it could be fully uttered. Twice Slo-cum sensed she had lost control, as she bucked and pelted, grinding her crotch against the rigid invader probing her most delicate regions.

And though she had promised to work to please him, Slocum watched with pleasure as an orgasm shook her body, sending a scarlet blush through the valley of her breasts and coaxing her nipples to stiff attention.

When her climax had ended, Sally Reed opened her emerald eyes and locked them firmly on the reclining John Slocum, pausing only momentarily in her pelvic gyrations.

"My God, you're still with me?" she gasped.

"Barely," Slocum answered honestly.

"Then hold on to your hat, John," she grunted, "'cause here's where I start to get good."

Sally Reed raised slightly off the bed to enable her longer, smoother thrusts at John Slocum's midsection. As each plunge became shorter in length and longer in duration, Slocum became aware of a clenching, gripping sensation. As he concentrated on the sensation, he felt a fluttering action, urging, milking his organ from the base to the tip.

It was too much for Slocum. Lightning struck at the base of his spine and traveled in a blinding, searing flash to explode between his ears. He was only vaguely aware of Sally's blissful cries echoing his own as he bucked and pumped his seed into her young body.

Later, when he felt capable of speech, Slocum said, "I think I'll have that drink now."

Sally Reed, still naked, carefully folded the note she'd just written into an envelope and tucked the flap down. "I don't have any sealing wax, so I guess I'll have to trust you. Actually, you can go ahead and read it if you want to."

"I don't read other people's mail," Slocum said, buckling his belt. "I don't peek through keyholes, either."

He took the letter and tucked it into his shirt pocket, promising himself that he would make every effort to find Sally's friend in his short time in Denver. She had truly made it worth his while.

"How will I recognize this Lottie when I see her?" he asked.

"She's beautiful," Sally answered. "Just look where the men are gathered and she's probably at the center. Wait. I have a photograph of her somewhere."

"A photograph?" Slocum was incredulous. "Where on earth did she get a photograph taken?"

Sally pulled open a bureau drawer. "A real funny character came through several months ago. Offered a lot of money to let him take pictures of us."

"French postcard?"

"Just photographs, any way we wanted. Well, what girl wouldn't want to see a photograph of herself? We would have done it for free, but . . . well, he did offer . . . "

"I understand."

"Here it is." Sally Reed pulled a curling photograph from the bottom of her bureau drawer and turned to hand it to Slocum. "I told you she was beautiful, and very high-class."

Slocum examined the photograph closely. Unlike most photographs he had seen, the subject in this one was smiling. It was indeed a face that would cause a man to take notice.

And it was a face Slocum recognized immediately.

14

They broke camp at mid-morning and started toward Apishapa Canyon.

Charlie Goodnight's herd was in prime shape. Goodnight, one of the pioneer cattlemen of the West, was in fine spirits. He was pleased with the influx of settlers into southern Colorado. Goodnight greeted Slocum with a slap on his back, led the wranglers to crude huts erected in the canyon.

While the crew rested, Slocum and Goodnight recalled some of their wilder moments during previous trail drives. When the men were out of sight, Slocum went to the chuck wagon and brought back the satchel of gold.

Goodnight was pleased that payment was being made in hard specie. "I hate that paper," he said. "Any crook can have some paper printed up, spread the stuff all over the territory. Some real talent would be needed to turn out fake gold pieces."

"These are straight from the Denver mint," Slocum said.

Goodnight pulled out a handful of the coins. They glittered in the sunlight.

"Dangnation! Those sure look pretty," said Goodnight.

They talked about Carlee Loving, the cattle business, the coming of the railroads to the West. Goodnight said that Chief Ouray and his Ute warriors were quiet. Slocum could expect an uneventful cattle drive to Cheyenne.

Following a day's rest, Slocum and the wranglers moved the herd out of Apishapa Canyon. They headed the cattle north and followed the traditional trail. Each night they took turns standing guard over the herd. During the day, Slocum rode point.

Slocum always hated the thought of a cattle drive. Then, when the herd started moving along the trail, he discovered a certain pleasure in the drive. A man had to be careful around a herd. A pistol shot, a rattlesnake, almost anything could spook a herd.

The cry of "Stampede!" was fearsome to wranglers. When a herd of cattle stampeded, the result was a loss of animals, work and danger. Every man knew of someone who had died under the hooves of a stampeding herd.

The weather was warm, the wind calm. Their journey was free from storms. The animals were docile, moving along with ease. Fred Tumwater and Jimmy Long were experts in watching for hazards. They were quick to move the animals away from any hazards on the trail.

Trouble came the night they camped a few miles south of Denver. Slocum and the men were resting after dinner. They were stretched out on the ground, their heads cradled by their saddles. Fred Tumwater and Earl Doolittle were out watching the herd. Carlos Rivera, the Mexican cook, was quietly washing up the dinner dishes.

Suddenly a bull bellowed in the twilight.

"He sounds frightened," Carlos said. "Maybe a wolf is coming to raid the herd."

Slocum stood up and brushed the dust off his pants. He saw a strange rider moving toward the herd. Even at that far distance, Slocum could see that the rider had a bandanna pulled up over the lower part of his face.

"Rustlers!" Slocum yelled. He rushed to saddle his horse.

"Redfern's bunch," snapped Jimmy Long. His voice was strained with anxiety.

From the front of the herd came the sound of gunfire.

Slocum spurred his horse foward. The animal was moving swiftly toward the herd.

A shotgun roared in the distance. The loud noise startled the herd. The cattle began to mill around, snorting and pawing the earth.

"Check on Doolittle!" Slocum yelled as Jimmy Long came riding up on his pinto. "I'll back up Tumwater."

They parted at the back of the herd.

Slocum's horse rushed past the cattle, cutting along the edge of the herd. Slocum reached down and pulled his Sharps repeating rifle from the scabbard.

Slocum looked for some sign of the rustlers. He caught sight of a rider trapped among a group of milling steers. Fred Tumwater was desperately trying to calm the cattle. He was attempting to hold the herd, not firing back at the four masked rustlers galloping toward him.

"Protect yourself!" Slocum yelled.

Tumwater's face was ghost-white in the twilight. He ducked as a bullet whizzed over his head.

Slocum snapped the rifle up to his shoulder. He squeezed off a quick shot at the masked riders. He had not taken the time to aim, but he was successful in drawing the rustler's attention away from Fred Tumwater.

The wild shot kicked up dust near the oncoming riders.

One masked man reined in, but the others kept charging toward the herd.

Slocum pulled back on the reins. His horse skittered to a quick stop and stood motionless. Slocum took careful aim and snapped off another round from the Sharps.

The rustler who had pulled up was knocked over the back of his horse. The animal pawed the earth, then took off into the growing darkness with an empty saddle.

Slocum pulled on the reins. His horse spun around. The three other riders were hooting, yelling, trying to get the herd to move. They carried blankets which they waved and snapped at the cattle.

Through the dimness, Slocum saw Fred Tumwater drop low in his saddle. The wrangler pulled his pistol and started to fire. A loud explosion echoed in the wilderness. Slocum saw orange flame spurt from the barrel of the rustler's pistol.

Tumwater fell off the side of his horse.

Slocum started to spur his horse forward, then saw that the other three rustlers had spun around. They were firing at Slocum, their guns roaring, bullets whizzing through the air.

Slocum swung out of the saddle. His horse went darting into a nearby grove of trees. Slocum took cover behind a large boulder. He pulled the Sharps repeater up into his familiar sniper position.

He squeezed the trigger. The gun roared and a rider dropped out of the saddle.

The remaining two riders were cutting away from the

herd. They spurred their mounts and vanished into the darkness.

Off to the left, where Jimmy Long had gone, Slocum heard gunfire and the muffled voice of a stranger.

"Pull out!" cried the rustler. "Every man for himself!"

Slocum slumped back as the sound of hooves indicated the rustlers were withdrawing.

He waited. The herd was settling down. Standing up, Slocum walked over to where Fred Tumwater had last been seen. The wrangler's horse was standing among a few steers. Fortunately, the animals had not trampled Tumwater, Slocum noticed. He bent down and looked at the ashen face.

Fred Tumwater was dead.

The rustler's bullet had gone into his right eye and emerged from the top of his head.

Slocum sighed.

Bracing himself, he pulled Tumwater's body away from the herd. He laid the body beside the grove of trees. He whistled for his horse. When the animal emerged out of the trees, Slocum laid Tumwater's body across the saddle. He picked up his rifle and walked back to camp leading the horse.

The other wranglers were in camp. Jimmy Long had gone through the raid without a scratch. Earl Doolittle was slumped up against a wagon wheel. He was bleeding from a shoulder wound. The Mexican cook, Carlos Rivera, was unbuttoning Doolittle's shirt.

Herb Morris was off by the side of the camp. Morris was trying to say something, but his lips moved silently. The cowboy's hands, arms, and legs were trembling in frantic involuntary movement.

Slocum went over to where Earl Doolittle was sitting. "You hurt bad?" Slocum asked.

The wrangler spoke through gritted teeth. "Hurts like hell," he said.

"Not too bad," said Carlos Rivera, coming back with a pan of hot water. "A flesh wound. Deep. The bullet's still in his shoulder. We should get him to a doctor as soon as possible."

Slocum bent down and inspected Doolittle's shoulder.

"Don't worry about it," he told the wrangler. "It will hurt like hell, but you are not going to die."

"I got the bastard who did it," said Jimmy Long. A hint of pride laced his voice. "Where's Fred?"

"I'm sorry," Slocum said. "He's dead, Jimmy."

A shocked melancholy infected the group. They spoke in low tones for the rest of the evening. Before turning in for the night, Slocum and Jimmy Long went out and brought back the bodies of the two rustlers. Left out in the open, the bodies would be attacked by night predators or trampled by the cattle.

They rose with the first hint of dawn the next morning. Rivera whipped up a quick breakfast of pancakes. Slocum and Jimmy Long went out and buried Fred Tumwater and the two rustlers. Tumwater was buried beneath a tall pine tree. Herb Morris fashioned a small cross with two sticks and a strip of rawhide for the head of the grave. The rustlers' graves were left unmarked. All were covered with stones to prevent wild animals from digging them up.

After a quick breakfast, they got the herd moving toward Denver. The men were grumbling about Tumwater's death, the fact that men like Bart Redfern could raid and plunder without being arrested.

Earl Doolittle rode up on the front of the chuck wagon during the remainder of the way to Denver. The herd moved easily during the morning. Around one o'clock in the afternoon, Slocum called a halt outside of Denver.

There was plenty of water along a small creek, where the grass was long and plentiful.

The crew wanted to keep the herd on grass for a couple of days.

Herb Morris expressed their viewpoint. "We ought to stay here, get rested up, then move on up to Cheyenne."

Slocum shook his head. "We're sitting on Bart Redfern's doorstep."

"What about the law?" asked Carlos Rivera.

Slocum patted the butt of his revolver. "This is it," he said.

"You want to keep going?" Carlos Rivera looked at Slocum as if the trail boss was clearly addled. "We need food. I only laid in enough for the trip back to Denver."

Before Slocum could answer, Earl Doolittle added, "I want to get to a sawbones."

Slocum nodded toward the wranglers. "We'll wait here while Carlos goes into town for supplies. While you're in town, drop Earl off at the doctor's office. On your way back, Carlos, pick up two good men who need work. You ought to be able to find two at the stockyards."

"No trouble doing that," answered the Mexican cheerfully.

"What about us?" asked Herb Norris.

"We stay here and guard the herd," Slocum told him.

"I ain't dying so you can make some money," grumbled Norris. "Give me and Doolittle our pay. I'm cashing out. I can tend cattle, but I sure as hell don't like people shooting at me."

"All right." Slocum pulled several gold pieces from his pocket. "You want to go with them, Jimmy?"

Jimmy Long shook his head. "I'll stick with you, John. No way am I gonna quit when the trail gets rough."

Herb Norris glared at Jimmy Long. "You'll be pushing

p daisies when I'm alive and well," he snapped.

"Well, they won't write 'coward' on my tombstone," immy Long retorted.

Herb Norris bristled, then controlled his temper with a hrug of his shoulders. "Every man does what he has to lo," he said, going off to get his horse.

A few minutes later, Slocum and Jimmy Long watched s Rivera, Norris, and Doolittle rode into town.

"Gonna seem a little lonely around here," said Long. "I lope Carlos gets back with some help."

"I think we can trust him," Slocum said.

"I've never been in a tight spot like this before."

"Enjoy the lull," said Slocum. "You never know what he future will bring."

The afternoon dragged along. Slocum and Long kept lose watch on the herd. They went out once and helped a ow who was undergoing a breech birth. The calf was a risky little animal once the ordeal of birth was over.

Slocum went over to the chuck wagon and rustled up ome hardtack.

Jimmy Long went down to the creek and came back vith a pail of fresh water.

They sat munching the hardtack and drinking water as he sun dropped lower in the west.

"I wonder what's taking Carlos so much time," said immy Long.

Slocum pointed toward the outskirts of Denver. "Two iders coming."

"Must be the men Carlos hired."

"Or somebody snooping after a herd," Slocum replied.

15

Slocum saw dust clouds being kicked up behind the herd. He squinted into the sun, saw a dozen riders headed directly for the cattle. He knew that something had happened in town, that this was Breedlow's play to rustle the herd. He recalled evesdropping at the bawdy house window. One of the men—Redfern, Needles, Thorne, or Ackerman—mentioned that one hundred thousand would be paid by the cattle buyer Bancroft when the herd passed the Platte River.

The first two horsemen came riding toward Slocum's camp.

"Better get up in the wagon," Slocum told Jimmy Long. "This looks like trouble. Stay hidden and cover me with one of those repeater rifles."

Without answering, Jimmy Long crawled into the chuck wagon.

"Watch your tail," Slocum said. "Don't do anything

foolish. I'll start the play. That's assuming there is something coming down."

"Okay," said Long. His voice was muffled by the canvas top of the wagon.

Slocum stood leaning against a wagon wheel. The riders continued toward the camp until, at a medium distance, Slocum discerned the figures of Jubal Thorne and Harold Ackerman. The hardcases were coming to settle scores and to pick up their blood money, he decided.

He waited.

Jubal Thorne and Harold Ackerman reined up about twenty-five yards from Slocum's wagon. The two men remained on their horses. The animals pawed the earth, made blowing sounds.

"You're riding those animals too fast," Slocum said.

"We couldn't wait to get out here, you pissant," said Jubal Thorne. "We'll be picking up a thousand dollars this afternoon, Slocum. All we have to do is nail your hide."

"That might be hard money to earn."

Ackerman laughed. "Hell, Slocum, I'd do it for free. I don't like nosy people who jump into everyone else's business. And I don't like looking at your ugly face around Denver. Time to clean up the town and let some handsome folks take center stage."

"Your play, boys," said Slocum.

"Let me take him." Jubal Thorne swung down out of the saddle. "I always wanted to try this rebel on a draw."

"You might get a surprise," Slocum snapped.

Jubal Thorne stepped away from his horse. Slocum kept shifting his gaze between Thorne and Ackerman. It was an old gunman's trick, but one that almost always worked. One man gets the victim's attention in what is supposed to be a fast-draw duel. The second man actually does the draw and kills the victim.

"You should have stayed out of Breedlow's business," said Thorne. He kept his hand high above his waist, above the big .44 Remington pistol that was holstered on his hip. "Breedlow doesn't like amateurs messing in his affairs."

"Breedlow?" Slocum snorted. "The real boss is Dave Needles."

Ackerman's face registered surprise. "How'd you know that?"

Ackerman looked down at Thorne, who was moving toward Slocum. Thorne's hand was slowly moving down toward his holstered pistol.

The horses snorted again.

The cattle began to mill around. Off behind him, Slocum heard Redfern's rustlers give yells to get the herd moving. Dust began to drift out of the grazing ground.

"We appreciate your work on our behalf," chuckled Thorne. "Not many men will go down to Apishapa Canyon and get a herd for our friends."

Leather creaked as Ackerman shifted in his saddle.

"Thorne, you gonna draw or just spend the day thinking about it?"

Thorne's gaze remained fixed on Slocum. "Let me do this my way," said the gunman.

Ackerman looked peeved. "I know, you're going to talk him to death."

"You're the one with the big mouth," Slocum told Ackerman.

"Little pissant!" Ackerman leaned forward in the saddle. His pistol hand was busy with the reins.

Without batting an eyelash, his face impassive, Slocum went into a draw. His hand moved faster than the eye could follow, a blurred streak of flesh that lifted his pistol from the holster.

Slocum's mind was now operating on instinct.

He saw Harold Ackerman's mouth drop open. The gunman's face registered surprise. Slocum went into a crouch. He squeezed off a shot in Ackerman's direction, then swung the gun at Jubal Thorne.

Thorne's hand was streaking toward his gun, but Slocum's bullet caught the gunfighter in the belly. Thorne was knocked back on the ground. His pistol went flying back in the grass.

Meanwhile, Jimmy Long was in the chuck wagon blasting away at both men. A rifle bullet tore into the side of Thorne's leg. Another shot entered Ackerman's chest right below the spot where Slocum's bullet had entered.

Harold Ackerman sat on his horse, staring at Slocum with dull eyes. As if his body was moving in slow motion, like time had stopped, Ackerman's hand moved toward his holstered pistol.

"Pissant!" screamed Ackerman. Bloody froth poured out of his mouth.

Ackerman's eyes glazed over and rolled back up into their sockets. He sat rigid for a moment. Then his body dropped off the horse and hit the ground. His right boot was caught in the stirrup, so Slocum walked over and undid the stirrup. Ackerman's leg plopped down on the ground. He was dead.

Slocum walked over to where Jubal Thorne was stretched out. Jimmy Long held a rifle at the dying gunfighter's head.

Jubal Thorne looked up at Slocum through pain-dulled eyes. "It wasn't supposed to happen this way." He coughed.

"I was supposed to let you draw first. Right?"

Thorne nodded. "Yes," he whispered hoarsely. "We had it all planned out."

"Sorry to disappoint you," said Slocum.

"Slocum . . ." Thorne's voice was a whimper. "I don't want to die."

A powerful coughing spasm racked Jubal Thorne's body. When the cough ended, Thorne's chest slumped and his head rolled over onto the right cheek.

Slocum stood up. The gunplay had taken only a few minutes, but the herd was already moving across the creek. In the distance, he could see Bart Redfern's men whistling to move the cattle along. Redfern had ten, maybe a dozen hands.

"You want to go after them?" asked Jimmy Long.

"We can't beat those odds," Slocum said. "Redfern's got too many men."

"I ain't letting them get away with it," snapped Long. "If you ain't going after them, I'll go alone."

Jimmy Long wheeled and started off to where the horses were hobbled in back of the chuck wagon.

Slocum grabbed the young wrangler's arm. "Hold up. We got more problems. Look at that new bunch of riders coming out from town."

Jimmy Long gazed toward Denver. He saw at least twenty riders moving at a rapid pace.

They were headed directly toward the camp.

16

Jimmy Long crawled back up into the chuck wagon. He reloaded the repeater rifle, poked the barrel through a tear on the side of the canvas top.

Slocum resumed his stance against the wagon wheel.

The riders were coming fast, faster than Jubal Thorne and Harold Ackerman had.

Slocum glanced off in the direction that Bart Redfern's men had taken the herd. All that could be seen were a couple of straggling calves. They had been unable to keep up when the herd was moved out at a swift pace. One calf was bawling, wandering around in search of the mother cow. The other calf just stood beside a bush, unmoving, unsure of what to do.

Slocum added cartridges to his pistol, spun the cylinder, and waited to get a better look at the riders.

They came into focus, strangers, a group of heavily armed men carrying rifles and shotguns.

Then Slocum grinned when the figure of Frank Bannerman—or was it Luther—came into view. A moment later, the other twin came out of the mass of riders. The twins took the lead of the group and spurred their horses forward.

Momentarily, the twins reined in their horses, looked down at the bodies of Harold Ackerman and Jubal Thorne.

"Trouble, huh?" said Frank Bannerman.

"You know there's trouble if you got dead bodies," Luther told his brother.

"They try to prod you?" Luther held a full-length double-barreled Greener shotgun across his lap.

"You might say that," Slocum answered.

Frank said, "Carlos Rivera came to the sheriff's office about an hour ago. He was slapped around by Thorne and Ackerman after they saw him buying supplies. Redfern got many men?"

"Had a dozen," Slocum replied.

"We'll fry their asses," snapped Luther. "Time we got rid of some of the murderin' trash collecting in Denver. Sheriff Fillmore rounded up this posse faster'n you can swat a fly."

By now the rest of the posse had pulled up to the chuck wagon. They were men of assorted sizes and weapons, riding horses and mules. Two men were even riding a buckboard pulled by a roan mare.

"All right, men," said Frank Bannerman. "I'm deputizing every dad-blast one of you. Right here. Ain't taking time to swear you in. Just mind that you're deputies of Sheriff Ben Fillmore. And the only thing we got to do is catch that bunch of cattle thieves."

"Dead or alive," Luther added.

"Preferably dead," said Frank. "The county don't like feeding prisoners."

"Let's go!" shouted one of the men on the buckboard.

The riders tore out across the creek, water splashing away from the animals' hooves.

"Wow!" said Jimmy Long. "I'd hate to have that bunch after me."

"The Bannerman boys may be talkers, but they're pretty good at handling things."

Slocum watched the posse ride after the rustling gang. Then he recalled that Bancroft had promised to pay one hundred thousand dollars to Manley Breedlow. The exchange was to be made when Bancroft saw the herd crossing the Platte River.

"I gotta go into town," Slocum said.

"I'll come along."

"It may get a little rough."

Long laughed. "What do you think it has been lately?"

They saddled their animals and headed toward Denver.

Slocum planned on warning Bancroft about Breedlow's treachery.

Slocum and Jimmy Long galloped into Denver. They tied their horses in front of the Brown Palace hotel. Slocum started into the building, then stopped.

He turned to Jimmy Long. "Go see Sheriff Ben Fillmore or the U.S. marshal. Marshal's name is Tom Jackson. Tell either of them that I'm going to warn the cattle buyer, Bancroft. It is possible that Bancroft won't believe me. I may need them to back up what I tell him."

Jimmy Long turned away and started moving down the wooden sidewalk.

"Jimmy!" Slocum yelled after the wrangler.

Long spun around.

"The sheriff's office is in the other direction." Slocum jerked his thumb over his shoulder.

Jimmy Long's face reddened. "Oh, yeah! Guess I'm pretty excited."

As Jimmy Long rushed away, Slocum went into the quiet, plush lobby of the Brown Palace hotel. He walked up to the desk and asked the clerk for Mr. Bancroft's room number.

The desk clerk raised his eyebrows at Slocum's appearance.

"Make it quick," said Slocum. "I got business with him."

"Mr. Ruben Bancroft is in suite two. Second floor," said the clerk.

Slocum crossed the lobby and went up the steps. Suite two was at the end of the hall. He knocked on the thick mahogany door.

The woman who had been in the lobby with Manley Breedlow opened the door. Slocum inhaled. She was one of the most beautiful women he had ever met. Her features were partially obscured by a silk scarf which she held against her right cheek.

"I'd like to talk with Ruben Bancroft," Slocum said.

"I'm Lily Bancroft, his daughter," the young woman said.

Slocum opened his mouth to speak, but instead said nothing.

"My father is indisposed. Maybe I can help you. Come in."

Slocum followed her into the lavish suite. The lighting was dim. Lily Bancroft led Slocum into a parlor.

"Have a chair," she said.

Slocum grinned sheepishly. "I've got too much dirt on me. I don't want to ruin the upholstery. I'll stand. Anyway, this won't take long."

"My goodness! You seem upset," said Lily Bancroft in an even, almost melodious voice.

"I am," Slocum said. "Your . . . father is about to get skinned of about a hundred thousand dollars."

"That can't be!" Lily Bancroft's eyes registered shock. "He's making a deal right now for some cattle. He's buying a herd from Manley Breedlow."

Slocum quickly related some of the details about the herd. "And about an hour ago," he concluded, "Bart Redfern's men rustled the herd. Now, Miss Bancroft, if you will tell me where your father is meeting Breedlow, perhaps we can stop the deal."

Lily Bancroft blinked at Slocum for a moment. She started to speak.

Slocum heard a door open behind him.

He whirled around as Manley Breedlow came into the room. Breedlow held a pistol in his right hand. The gun was pointed directly at John Slocum's chest.

"It won't be necessary for you to see Ruben," Breedlow said.

Lily Bancroft began to cry. She moved the silk scarf and Slocum caught sight of the bruise on her cheek.

"What the hell is going on here?" Slocum asked.

"You're not much of a detective," Manley Breedlow sneered. "You got part of it right, Slocum, but just part of it. Those cattle are going to Cheyenne, only you don't get paid for the herd."

The door on the opposite side of the room opened. Slocum's mouth dropped open when Carlee Loving walked into the parlor. She was dressed in a leather skirt and boots, an outfit a woman would wear on the trail.

"What're you doing here?" Slocum demanded.

"Making money," Carlee said. "Lots of money. Right, Manley?"

Breedlow smiled. "That's right, darling."

"That money you took to Charlie Goodnight didn't come from the mint," Carlee told Slocum. "Ruben Bancroft paid for the herd in advance. I've got forty-five thousand sitting in the other room in another bag."

Slocum's mind reeled. The fact that Carlee Loving was involved with Breedlow and his cronies seemed unreal.

Slocum said, "I think I'm getting the drift. You get a hundred thousand from Bancroft."

"That's right," Carlee smiled.

"You give me forty-five thousand to get the herd and bring it up here."

"You can see the money involved," answered Carlee.

"You sell the herd for sixty-five thousand, which delivers a twenty thousand profit. So, altogether you get a hundred and sixty-five thousand, minus the sixty-five thousand paid for the cattle."

"You got a part of it," Manley Breedlow growled. "You won't live long enough to find out the rest."

Slocum knew he had to start moving fast. He looked over at Carlee Loving.

"I really didn't give a damn," he said. "If you had told me all of this in the beginning, then I wouldn't have got involved. Why did you set me up?"

"I didn't," said Carlee. "I made the bid, backed you because we stood to make a little money. When Manley couldn't force you out, he had you followed to my place. We got to talking. Manley told me the stakes that were involved. I agreed to help him. Now, John, I'll make a great deal of money, Manley makes money, and there's no end to it."

Slocum began to see the greed, the hypocrisy, the vicious nature of Carlee Loving. She had been driven by the desire for money since her childhood. Now that grasping nature had gotten her involved with Manley Breedlow. She was in over her head. Breedlow had a big scheme set up. It might have worked if Redfern got away with the herd.

"Maybe it isn't too late for you, John," Carlee said. "Do you want to throw in with Manley and me?"

"Hell," Slocum answered, "it beats dying broke."

Breedlow shook his head. "No, Carlee. Slocum is the perfect choice to take the blame for this. You can tell the sheriff that you backed him, that he twisted things around by making the bid in his name. Those are your cattle out there. Slocum is a con man who was taking advantage of your innocent nature."

"I got to admire your mind," Slocum told Breedlow.

Manley Breedlow moved a step forward. Slocum noticed that Breedlow's feet were solidly planted on a small area rug.

"It is something of a grand—"

Breedlow saw Slocum dive for the floor.

Breedlow squeezed off a shot as Slocum grabbed the end of the rug, jerking it out from under him.

The shot went wild and plunked into the wall of the suite. Lily Bancroft picked up a heavy lead crystal ashtray and threw it at Carlee Loving. Then Lily roiled up out of her chair and went at Carlee Loving tooth and claw. Carlee screamed and began to fight back.

Slocum pounced on Breedlow when the man hit the floor. Breedlow shuffled around trying to grab the pistol he had dropped during his fall. Once, twice, Slocum slammed a fist into Breedlow's face. Then they were locked in each other's arms, squeezing and struggling, rolling over the floor of the suite.

Manley Breedlow brought up his hand, slammed his palm against Slocum's nose. Blood gushed out.

Manley made a quick maneuver and moved away. He rolled over to where the pistol lay on the carpet. His fingers tightened on the butt and found the trigger.

Breedlow brought the gun around as Slocum rolled against him. They struggled with every ounce of available strength. Breedlow urged the pistol barrel down against Slocum's ear.

"So long, you bastard!"

Breedlow's finger tightened on the trigger.

Slocum rolled back. His hand tightened against Breedlow's wrist, snapping the arm back.

The gun roared.

Manley Breedlow looked dumbfounded.

Slocum began to rise up off the floor.

He looked down at Breedlow, who had shot himself between the eyes. Breedlow was dead.

Slocum walked over to where Lily Bancroft and Carlee Loving were wrestling on the floor. He was about to intervene when Lily landed a hard right cross to Carlee's temple. Miss Loving was down and out for the count.

Lily stood up. She adjusted her clothing.

"Where's your . . . Ruben?" Slocum asked.

"Tied up in the other room," Lily said.

At that moment there was the sound of boots outside the suite. The door opened and Jimmy Long, Sheriff Ben Fillmore, and U.S. Marshal Tom Jackson rushed into the room.

"Take care of this mess," said Slocum. "I got to see

Dave Needles about a few things."

Sheriff Fillmore nodded. "We'll clean up. The boys saved the herd. The Bannermans killed every one of those rustlers."

Slocum grinned. "I know. The county doesn't like to—"

"They're good boys," said the sheriff.

Slocum found Dave Needles sitting in the back of a Larimer Street saloon. The cattle buyer for the Union Pacific Railroad was hunched over a bottle of authentic Kentucky bourbon whiskey. He was smoking a long black cheroot.

Slocum walked up to the cattle buyer. "Breedlow's not coming," he told Needles.

Needles looked up with a startled expression. For an instant his face sagged. Then, moving quickly, Dave Needles leaped out of his chair and started running for the back door. Slocum grabbed the back of the cattle buyer's jacket and pulled him back into the chair.

Needles sat quietly, staring sullenly at the floor.

Sheriff Ben Fillmore and U.S. Marshal Tom Jackson came into the saloon.

"Jesus, you move fast," said Jackson.

"Is this jasper involved?" asked Fillmore.

"Gentlemen, this is Dave Needles," said Slocum. "He is the cattle buyer for the Union Pacific Railroad. Mr. Needles worked with Manley Breedlow to squeeze out the other cattle brokers. Then, when Needles handed in the bids from Breedlow, he doubled the amount. So he got a split from Breedlow and took another big portion for himself. And there was plenty of money to go around. The company is so busy laying rail that a deal like this could operate undetected. Right, Needles?"

Dave Needles continued to stare at the floor.

Slocum went on. "It was a slick operation until Breed-low decided to pull a big double-cross. He wanted the money *and* the cattle."

The cattle buyer looked up at the lawman with a pained expression. "Do I have to sit here and listen to these fairy tales?" he asked. "I don't care how many yarns Slocum spins, I don't want to be forced to listen to them."

"How about the Tucker boys?" asked Slocum. "I shot one in the alley, but it must have been a woman who killed the other one out by the stockyards."

"No," said Needles.

"Who, then?"

Needles started to speak. Then he clamped his mouth shut and stared past Slocum and the lawmen.

"Well, here's Mr. Bancroft and Lily," said Tom Jackson.

Ruben Bancroft came close to the table where Dave Needles was sitting. Without speaking, Bancroft pulled his hand out of his pocket. He held a small revolver. He pulled the trigger. Sheriff Ben Fillmore went down.

Slocum had started to react to this shooting when Lily Bancroft slipped a derringer out of her purse. She pointed the gun at point-blank range. Dave Needles was killed instantly by the bullet that smashed through his brain.

Slocum spun around, grabbed Lily Bancroft and pried the gun out of her hand.

"What in hell is going on?" Slocum demanded. The young woman struggled to pull away from his grip.

Meanwhile, U.S. Marshal Tom Jackson had forced Bancroft to drop his weapon.

Slocum glared at the cattle broker. "You were the mastermind behind the whole thing," he said. "I've seen you somewhere before, mister."

Sheriff Ben Fillmore got up from the floor. He held his

and over the wound in his arm. "I'm just winged," he
said. He jerked his head in Bancroft's direction. "He used
to be a partner with Chisholm. He was kicked out when
Chisholm caught him cheating on the count."

Slocum remembered seeing Ruben Bancroft in Dodge
City. He recalled that Bancroft knew everything about the
cattle business except how to make a profit.

"Too bad, Bancroft," said Slocum. "People like you
spoil everything. Carlee Loving was a good woman until
you and Breedlow dangled money in front of her. Dave
Needles might have lived a long and useful life if he hadn't
been pulled into your operation. But your kind always
comes along and ruins everything. And then, of course,
there's your so-called daughter."

Bancroft snarled. "Slocum, you're a dumb fool. You're
dumb enough to believe that Lily is my daughter. She's just
a high-class whore I picked up in Trinidad. Expensive, but
she satisfies my whims."

"Lottie Catron, isn't it?" Slocum asked and was pleased
with the surprised looks he drew from the woman and
Bancroft. "Remind me to deliver a message to you from a
mutual friend."

Suddenly Ruben Bancroft made a lunge and pulled
away from Tom Jackson's grip.

Bancroft's hand shot up his sleeve.

The hideout pistol came into view as Slocum pulled the
trigger on his sixgun.

Ruben Bancroft fell back over a chair, dead.

The woman he had called Lily began to cry.

Slocum took her by the shoulder. "There's just one thing
to clear up," he said. "Who killed the kid out by the stockyards?"

"Carlee Loving did it," the woman sobbed. "It was to

prove that we could trust her."

Slocum swore.

Sheriff Fillmore said, "You ever think of being a law man, Slocum?"

"Not a hell of a lot, Ben. In fact, never."

JAKE LOGAN

J.D. HARDIN

"THE MOST EXCITING WESTERN WRITER SINCE LOUIS L'AMOUR" —JAKE LOGAN

__07700-4	CARNIVAL OF DEATH #33	$2.50
__08013-7	THE WYOMING SPECIAL #35	$2.50
__07257-6	SAN JUAN SHOOTOUT #37	$2.50
__07259-2	THE PECOS DOLLARS #38	$2.50
__07114-6	THE VENGEANCE VALLEY #39	$2.75
__07386-6	COLORADO SILVER QUEEN #44	$2.50
__07790-X	THE BUFFALO SOLDIER #45	$2.50
__07785-3	THE GREAT JEWEL ROBBERY #46	$2.50
__07789-6	THE COCHISE COUNTY WAR #47	$2.50
__07974-0	THE COLORADO STING #50	$2.50
__08088-9	THE CATTLETOWN WAR #52	$2.50
__08669-0	THE TINCUP RAILROAD WAR #55	$2.50
__07969-4	CARSON CITY COLT #56	$2.50
__08743-3	THE LONGEST MANHUNT #59	$2.50
__08774-3	THE NORTHLAND MARAUDERS #60	$2.50
__08792-1	BLOOD IN THE BIG HATCHETS #61	$2.50
__09089-2	THE GENTLEMAN BRAWLER #62	$2.50
__09112-0	MURDER ON THE RAILS #63	$2.50
__09300-X	IRON TRAIL TO DEATH #64	$2.50
__09213-5	HELL IN THE PALO DURO #65	$2.50
__09343-3	THE ALAMO TREASURE #66	$2.50
__09396-4	BREWER'S WAR #67	$2.50
__09480-4	THE SWINDLER'S TRAIL #68	$2.50
__09568-1	THE BLACK HILLS SHOWDOWN #69	$2.50
__09648-3	SAVAGE REVENGE #70	$2.50
__09714-5	TRAIN RIDE TO HELL #71	$2.50
__09784-6	THUNDER MOUNTAIN MASSACRE #72	$2.50
__09895-8	HELL ON THE POWDER RIVER #73	$2.75

Available at your local bookstore or return this form to:

THE BERKLEY PUBLISHING GROUP
Berkley • Jove • Charter • Ace
THE BERKLEY PUBLISHING GROUP, Dept. B
390 Murray Hill Parkway, East Rutherford, NJ 07073

Please send me the titles checked above. I enclose _____. Include $1.00 for postage and handling if one book is ordered; add 25¢ per book for two or more not to exceed $1.75. CA, IL, NJ, NY, PA, and TN residents please add sales tax. Prices subject to change without notice and may be higher in Canada. Do not send cash.

NAME_____

ADDRESS_____

CITY_____ STATE/ZIP_____

(Allow six weeks for delivery.)